BLACK WHITE LETCHERY
VOLUME 1

Will Buster

BLACK WHITE LETCHERY
VOLUME 1

4PLAY PRESS

CONTENTS

Bad Cop Good Cop

My name is Keoki Townsend and I'm married to my wonderful husband Robert since 5 years back.

I am of Japanese descent as you might have guessed from my first name. My parents moved here about 40 years ago, so I'm born and raised here in the states.

For a living I work as a police officer, a sergeant actually. I've been doing this for the past seven years.

My husband Robert lost his job a couple of weeks ago so now we only have my pay check to live on.

Because of this our house payments are behind. And if he's not able to get a job soon we might be forced to move. But I'm sure we'll get the money somehow.

Let me tell you a little more about myself.

I'm 31 years old, about 5 feet 5 inches tall and I have long black hair. I have quite a slender body, long smooth legs and a thin waist.

I'm quite proud of my still rather perky C size breasts. They are very full, firm and soft. My butt I think fits rather nice with the rest of my body, not too big and not too small.

For a while now I've been heading up a police task force with the purpose of getting enough evidence to place a specific gang behind bars. This gang is a rather small one but the members are very careful so we haven't been able to arrest them yet. Normally a small gang like this doesn't get a task force assigned to them, but this gang is a bit different. They have recently taken over most of the drug related business in our city. The leader of the gang is one, Jermaine Carls. As with the rest of the gang members he is black.

A few days ago we got a tip that in one of the gangs hangouts there would be a few kilos of illegal drugs. So this could be our chance to arrest some of the gang members. So here we were, outside their hangout ready to move in. As I was the head of the task force it was my decision when we would move in.

I checked with the other officers on the car radio. "Williams, is your group ready?" I asked officer Williams over the radio. "Yes we are, just waiting for you to say when." He replied.

"Billings, is your group ready?"

"Yes ma'am, we are ready to go." He told me.

"Ok, on the count of 5 we move in." I gave the order.

I counted down. "5, 4, 3, 2, 1 GO."

Myself and the rest of the officers then got out of our cars and began to run towards the hangout. When we got up to the doors into the building, we stopped and rammed down the doors and then we ran inside. "Police! Get down!" We yelled upon entry. There were four guys inside and we got them down on the floor and handcuffed them quickly. We then proceeded to search the place for the drugs. We searched for a few hours but we couldn't find anything.

"Sergeant Townsend, we have finished the search of the last room." One of the officers reported to me.

"And?" I asked with a cynical grin on my face.

"We didn't find it."

"Ok, let's wrap it up for today. We'll take the four guys in for questioning and see if they tell us something."

After the last of the task force had driven away, I decided to stay and see If I could find something we might have missed. I just couldn't believe that we hadn't found anything. I searched and searched but I couldn't find anything either. So I decided to rest for a while, so I sat down on a couch.

When I sat down, I thought the pillow I sat down on felt rather strange. I grabbed the pillow and shook it a few times. It sounded like there was something inside of it. I decided to open up the pillow. So I took out my pocket knife and cut it open.

"Jesus H Christ!"

The pillow was full of money. It had to be nearly fifty grand inside of it.

I then checked the rest of the pillows, but there was no more money in any of them. But I must say that I was a little disappointed about that there was only money inside of it. We couldn't put these guys away just for having some money in their pillow.

If it only could have been the damned drugs. I guess I'll go down to the station and put the money in as evidence. But then I thought of something crazy. Robert and our house payments. With this money we could make our payments and keep our house. No one in the force knows about this money. "I could just walk out with the money and no one would know." I thought to myself. On the other hand, it was Illegal. It wasn't my money. However, I didn't want to lose our house either. I thought about it for a while, then I decided to take it. I could always put the money in our bank vault box and use the money slowly and carefully. I grabbed the pillow and walked out to my squad car and drove away.

A week past by and no one at the station had said anything about any money, and my task force just regarded last week's raid as a bust. So I finally decided that I would go to the bank and make our house payments with the money I had found.

A few days later when my husband asked about how our bills had gotten paid, I lied to him and told him that I had inherited some money from a distant relative that had died.

Then one day when I was patrolling in my squad car and I stopped to get some coffee something happened. When I got back to my car and got in, Jermaine the gang leader was sitting in the other seat. "What the hell do you think you're doing here?" I yelled has I reached for my gun.

But Jermaine had already aimed his gun in my face. "Now listen up bitch." I know you stole my money a week ago when you raided our hangout."

"No I didn't." I said, feeling quite scared. "Don't lie, one of my guys saw you leaving our place with a pillow." "Oh god, what am I going to do." I thought to myself. "And I also know that you have paid the bank with the money." "If I told this to your police internal affairs, you would go to prison. So you have no choice but to do what I say."

He was right, if he told them and they checked my bank accounts they would know that he was telling the truth. And I would most likely go to jail for a long time. The best case scenario would be that I would lose my job and get house arrest. "What do you want?"

"First I want you to keep your police away from my business."

"I don't have the power to do that."

"You'll find some way to lead them away from me." He told me as he pressed his gun against the side of my head.

"Ok." I said thinking that he might shoot me otherwise.

"And I want you to meet me tomorrow at noon at this address."

"What for?"

"What do you think? I want some of that pussy of yours."

"No I can't, please I'm married." I actually pleaded.

"Be there tomorrow, or I'll tell the D.A. about the money." Then he got out of the car and walked away. I sat there to the end of my shift thinking about what I would do. But I couldn't come up with anything, if I didn't do what he said he would tell my superiors and I would go to prison. And there was the other thing he told me to do. To go to this address and then let him fuck me. I felt disgusted by the idea of it, and I really didn't want to do that to my husband. But I had little choice but to do what he said.

The next day I was out on patrol and it was getting closer to noon. I knew I had to go to that address he gave so I drove over to it. It turned out to be a motel. The note with the address he gave me also had a room number on it.

So I got out of my car and walked over to the motel room. I was feeling both embarrassed and humiliated as I knocked on the door.

"Come in." Someone said from the other side. I then walked in.

The room looked like your average motel room with a big bed in the middle.

Jermaine was sitting on a chair beside the bed as I walked in.

"Well officer have you come to arrest me?" I didn't reply.

"No, then you must be here for something else." Jermaine then stood up and walked over to me after I shut the door.

"Get your hands up." He told me.

I felt even more humiliated as I raised my hands over my head.

Jermaine then got behind me.

"I've always wanted to fuck a police woman." He told me as he reached around and grabbed my breasts and started to squeeze them through my uniform. "Lets get this uniform off of you."

With my hands over my head, he unbuckled my weapon belt and threw it on the floor. He then began to undo my police blouse. When he had removed my blouse he quickly undid my bra.

"Wow bitch you have some really nice tits." He said as he was squeezing my breasts rather roughly. "Now get your pants off." I reluctantly lowered my hands and pulled down my pants and stepped out of them. "And your panties." I removed my panties. "Now turn around."

I turned around and faced him.

He had removed all of his clothes except for his underwear.

"Now officer, get down on your hands and knees and crawl over here." He ordered. I felt totally humiliated as I got down on my knees and crawled over to him.

When I got over to him he placed his hand on my head and pulled me so I had my face close to him and facing his crotch.

"Now pull my underwear down." I reached up and grabbed his underwear and pulled them down. And out popped this huge hard black cock. It had to be at least 12 inches long. I couldn't help staring at it, even though I was disgusted by the very sight of Jermaine's tool.

Jermaine then grabbed his cock and began to rub it in my face.

"Now open that sweet mouth of yours." I really didn't want to, but I didn't know what else to do.

I opened my mouth and he then stuck that big cockhead of his into my open mouth. I felt that thing of his as he placed it on my tongue.

"Suck it, you police whore."

If someone had called me anything like that on the street I would have punched him out. But I couldn't do that here so I reluctantly began to suck his cock.

"Ahh yeah bitch, that's good." He said as I was sucking his cock. I couldn't believe I was doing this, having this criminals black cock in my mouth. I had only given my husband a few blowjobs before this degrading event. Jermaine then grabbed my head and began to push his cock deeper into my throat.

"Let's see how much you can take."

I soon began to gag on it but he still pushed a bit more of it into my throat and then he pulled it out. I was coughing trying to catch my breath.

"Damn you almost deep throated me, no one had ever gotten that much in Before. I knew you were going to be a real slut." He was grinning.

I looked up at his huge black cock and I was in disbelief that I had almost gotten that whole thing down my throat. What was I thinking, I was disgusted by this and still I felt myself getting wet between my legs.

Jermaine then pulled me up and carried me over to the bed and laid me down on it. "Now I'm going to have me some of that police pussy." He got on top of me and started to kiss me. And soon to my surprise I felt his tongue inside of my mouth, I had actually opened my mouth and was kissing him.

And just as I realized this and tried to close my mouth, he shoved his big cock inside of my pussy.

"Ohhhh godddd." I found myself screaming out loud. He began to fuck me with almost all of his length. I couldn't believe it, but I was actually moaning. "Damn, you have a fucking tight pussy." He growled.

"I bet you haven't felt anything like this before, you Asian slut." No I hadn't but I didn't want to tell him that. As he was slamming his huge cock inside of me I started to feel something I rarely feel when having sex.

I was actually getting closer and closer to having an orgasm. "No I can't cum with this guy. That is something that I only want to do with Robert." I thought to myself.

But there was nothing to stop it now, I was too close. "Ohhhh godddd yessss." I moaned out as I was cumming hard. And for a second I forgot who was fucking me. I was actually having an orgasm with this guy whom I despised. Soon after this Jermaine started to grunt louder and louder. And a moment later he pulled out of me and got up to my face. I looked over at his cock and soon his white gooey sperm hit me in the face.

He was spurting more and more cum. It felt as if I had sperm all over my face. I actually got some of it inside my mouth.

It tasted funny, I had never had a guy cum in my mouth before. I then spat it out.

Jermaine's cock was now only dripping out cum. He started to smear his sperm all over my face with his cock. "That's how a slut should look after having a good fuck." He actually laughed. "But don't let me catch you spitting any of it out in the future." "Ok." I told him reluctantly. Before he left me in the hotel room, he gave me another address and told me to be there after my shift on Friday and to wear my uniform.

The days that followed I wanted to tell my husband but I couldn't, I didn't want to lose him. However, I did start taking birth control pills to play it safe. So when Friday came, after my shift I went to the address Jermaine had given me.

And this time it was an apartment building. There was also a number 24 written down on the note he gave me.

It had to be an apartment room so I went up to room 24, and knocked on the door. Someone said come in so I went inside. When I had closed the door behind me I was shocked at what I saw. In the room there were five black guys sitting on a couch and a couple of chairs. One of them was Jermaine. "And here she is guys, our very own police stripper." Jermaine announced. "Wait a minute, I'm not going to sleep with all of you." I told them. "No you're not, but because you spat out my cum in the motel room you are going to give us all blowjobs and then swallow all of our loads." Jermaine informed me. "I don't." I tried to say something.

"But first you're going to strip for us." Jermaine interjected. I hesitated for a moment. "I told you to strip." Jermaine said in an angry voice. So I began to slowly unbutton my blouse.

I had never taken my clothes off in front of a bunch of guys before. A moment later I had removed my blouse and began to slowly undo my pants.

"Yeah baby, get those pants off." One of the guys yelled out. "Yeah I wanna see your ass." Another one said.

As I pulled off my pants I saw that the guys began to take their clothes Off as well. They had soon removed all of their clothes, and then they sat back down and began to slowly stroke their cocks as I was stripping. I had now undone my bra and let it fall to the ground.

"M m m, those are some nice tits." One of them said. I was actually having mixed emotions about this. On one hand I was feeling rather humiliated for having to do this. But on the other hand I was getting rather turned on by having all these guys cheer me on as I was stripping.

"Now get those panties off, I want to see some pussy." Another one said.

I reached down and started to pull down my panties.

"Yeah turn around and bend over, lets see some ass." Jermaine chuckled. So I turned around and then I leaned forward showing those black guys my ass and my pussy.

Then one of the guys came over to me. "I have something for you." He said holding his cock in his hand. I looked down at it, it wasn't as long as Jermaine's but I think it was a bit thicker. "Suck it." He ordered. I got down on my knees and reached out and grabbed it. It felt a bit heavy as I had it in my hand. And I couldn't even get my hand around it, it was too thick. Then I reached over and began to suck on its big cockhead. I had to open my mouth quite widely to be able to get it in.

"Oh yeah baby, suck it." He grunted. I was stroking it as I sucked that fat black cock of his. I could taste his precum leaking out from his hard cock. I was actually getting into this and soon I was sucking him rather heavily.

"Ahhh yeah baby yeah." And soon I felt a splash hit the back of my throat. He was cumming.

I could taste stream after stream of his hot sperm as he was shooting it into my mouth. He was cumming so much that I had no other choice but to swallow it. To my surprise it actually didn't taste all that bad.

"That's right bitch, swallow my load." The guy grunted.

After this guy had stopped cumming, I was told to come over to the couch where the other three guys were sitting. I walked over there and then got down on my knees between the legs of the guy who was sitting in the middle.

He also had a long and thick cock. I was amazed at how big all of these guys were. Then I began to suck the guy in the middle. The other guys actually stood up and were standing next to me on each side. I now had three big black cocks right next to my face. So I began to switch between them, sucking one guy for a minute then another.

As I was sucking one cock I was stroking the other two. They felt really big in my hands. I was now really slurping on the guy in the middle. And soon I noticed that he began to really tense up.

A second later he shot his load right into my mouth. I continued to suck him as he was cumming. I tried to swallow all of his cum but some leaked out through my lips.

As the guy eased up and stopped cumming, one of the other guys got his cock up to my lips. I knew he was about to cum so I quickly put my lips around his cock. I was right, as soon as I got my lips around it he came.

He spurted wad after wad of sperm into my mouth. This guy tasted a bit sweeter than the other two guys had. I actually found myself liking the taste of their cum.

The third guy couldn't hold until I was finished with the other guy so he began to cum right in my face.

As I noticed this I opened my mouth wide so that both of the guys could cum inside of me. "This one is a real cum junkie." One of the guys said.

"Yeah she's a real slut." The other one said.

As both of them stopped cumming I soon realized that Jermaine was left.

Jermaine was sitting in his chair with his rock hard cock in his hand.

So I crawled over to him. "So you want to suck my black cock do you?" I realized that I was actually nodding. "Then tell me you want it bitch."

"I really want your black cock." The strange thing was that I really wanted to suck him.

"Then go right ahead." So I leaned over and took his big cock into my mouth. I was soon bobbing my head up and down over it.

As he had waited the longest for me to suck him he couldn't hold it back very long, and soon he shot his load. He came hard inside my mouth. I swallowed all of his cum as his pace slowed down. I continued to suck him clean until he had completely stopped cumming. "I told you police women make great sluts." Jermaine told the guys. They nodded and laughed. "Now get dressed and get the hell out of here."

I quickly got dressed and got out of there. As I was driving home I couldn't believe that I had given all those guys blowjobs and then swallowed all of their cum.

The weekend went by and I came home from another Mondays patrolling on the streets.

"Oh honey is that you." Robert asked.

"Yes it's me." "Good, I was about to check out this video tape I found on the door step earlier." "You want to see it with me?" He asked.

"Ok." I wondered what could be on it. Robert inserted the tape into the VCR and hit play.

The video started by a woman opening a door and coming into a room.

"That looks a bit like you Keoki." Robert said.

It actually did look a little like me. The woman was also wearing a police uniform.

As we continued to watch, the woman on the tape started to strip. It then hit me, it was me on that tape. Jermaine had had somebody videotape my strip for those guys last Friday. "I don't think we should watch this." I told Robert. "Why not? It's just getting good." A moment later he seemed to realize that he knew the person on the tape.

"My god Keoki, that's you!"

I looked down on the floor almost starting to cry. As my husband continued to watch the tape he saw me getting down on my knees and giving this black guy a blowjob.

"How could you fucking do this?" He asked me in an angry voice.

I started to explain the situation to him. "So that's how you got the money to pay off our house payments." Robert said.

"Yes."

When I had explained everything to him he stood up. "Well Keoki, If you want to stay married to me you are going to have to stop doing what this guy tells you to do. And then you're going to tell your police captain about this blackmail." Robert informed me.

"But honey I might go to prison." "Well you can't keep doing this and the captain is a friend of ours, he might be able to make a deal for you, especially if you can help the department nail this bastard."

"Ok."

I didn't want to lose Robert, he's the love of my life. So I agreed to tell the captain. The next day I was going down to the station to tell the captain. "Robert I love you." I told him as I was leaving. "We'll see." Once I had arrived at the station, I told the captain the whole story. "I'm a little disappointed in you sergeant Townsend." The captain said. But then he started to explain that under the circumstances he might be able to convince the District Attorney to look between his fingers for this one time. "Why would he do that?"

The captain then told me that they had gotten a tip, that Jermaine and his gang was going to be receiving the largest load of illegal drugs this city has ever seen. And he told me that the police chief really wants to get them while they are receiving it. "So Townsend, if you can get the location for the drug meet then you might be off the hook."

"Do you think that they will really let this pass?"

"Well both the police chief and the District Attorney is up for re-election this year, so if we could get this gang and the drugs, it would be huge."

"Yeah I see your point." "But this would mean you would be going back to Jermaine."

"Well I don't think I have much choice." I told him. I did give him the address and apartment number I had visited the previous Friday, just in case it mattered.

A few days later I got a call from Jermaine. He told me to meet him at a place.

This time it was a very nice apartment building. I went up to the room he had given me the number to, after I had informed the Captain about this new address.

When I went inside Jermaine told me that this was his own apartment. An hour later when he had slept with me and I was getting ready to leave Jermaine got a phone call. He told me to leave and went into the next room to answer it. As he answered the phone I picked up the phone in this room and listened to what they were saying.

It was a guy giving Jermaine the address for a drop. I wrote down the address and then I left before Jermaine got back, so he would think that I had left before the guy gave him the address. The day of the drop SWAT teams had surrounded the address that I had gotten.

And soon Jermaine and his gang showed up. Soon after this a large truck drove up.

Jermaine and another guy was standing behind the truck talking. The other guy was showing Jermaine the inside of the truck, and he was also giving him a sample of something white.

It was the drug shipment.

The captain gave the order and the SWAT team moved in. There was some Gun-fire, but in minutes, the SWAT had arrested all of them.

Jermaine and the gang all got 20 years or more in prison.

The captain was right, the District Attorney and the Chief of Police both looked the other way regarding my case. But I still got disciplined by the captain. I was suspended for six months without pay and after that I was put on desk duty for a year. On the home front, Robert eventually forgave me. Actually our sex life has improved a great deal after this.

But I was surprised to find the video tape of me with those black guys in one of Robert's drawers. He had actually kept it and had been watching it a lot. I guess he was getting turned on by watching it. Oh Well!

Banging The Boxer

Myron Flarity has quite a nice life. He works as a financial manager for a heavy weight boxer. He earns quite a good living doing this, but he has always spend his money rather quickly so he has always needed more of it.

In his personal life he's happily married to a gorgeous woman since three years back. Her name is Cassie and she used to be a model but she quit working a year after they got married.

When she was a model she was in a lot of magazines. Though she never posed nude.

Myron has been the envy of a lot of guys because of Cassie. And the day she said yes, Myron was the happiest man alive.

Needless to say, Cassie has a great body.

Cassie is a perfect blonde. She is 28 years old and about 5 feet 8 inches tall. She's got a thin waist and a very slim body. Her breasts are a size B. They are very firm and soft, along with nice big nipples. She also has an awesome ass. It's really firm and matches the rest of her.

Myron himself is rather skinny and has an average look. And he's 32 years old.

The man Myron works for has won most of his professional fights so he's quite rich. He has quite a few managers, medics and trainers on his pay role, Myron being the only white man of them.

The fighter's name is Tyrone and in the ring he's called the tank, because nothing rarely stops him. He's a dark, black male and about 6 feet 3 inches tall. Tyrone isn't called the tank for nothing, his body is all muscle. Hitting him in the stomach is like hitting a brick wall. Tyrone has an office above a gym that he owns where Myron works. But Myron often has to drive over to Tyrone's place to get him to sign financial papers and such things. Tyrone's place is actually the penthouse floor in an exclusive Hotel. On that floor he has his own private gym, a swimming pool and two smaller heated pools, so he has a really great place there.

The Tank also has a few close friends who almost always are there and of course his personal manager Jermaine.

***

Lately Myron has been thinking about a way to get his hands on a large sum of cash using Tyrone's money.

A man Myron had met in a bar a month ago who works as a consultant at a small technology company, had told him about a piece of hardware that the company had developed and was about to release.

It was a revolutionary piece of hardware that the company was about to launch and whoever owned a lot of stock in the company would make millions.

Being Tyrone's financial manager Myron had access to Tyrone's money.

Today was Monday and Myron was sitting in his office talking to his new buddy Thomas about the deal.

"Are you sure about this company." Myron asked Thomas.

"Yes I'm sure, I only told you about it because I like to think of you as a friend." Thomas replied.

"How much do you have invested in the company?" Myron asked.

"About $200 000." Thomas said.

"That's a lot." Said Myron.

"I might be able to get my hands on $100 000." Myron told Thomas.

"Well the more you invest the more you will earn."

"How much do you think their stock will go up?" Myron asked.

"Well about ten times." Thomas said.

"That much, but $100 000 is all that I can "borrow"." Myron told Thomas.

"When to you think you will have the money." Thomas asked.

"I can have it in two days." Myron replied with certainty.

"Well you need to buy their stock within a week because next Monday they will launch their product." Thomas warned Myron.

"Where can I buy their stock?" Myron asked.

"Well either you can go to this stock broker and ask them to buy it for you." Thomas handed Myron the name of the stock broker.

"Or you can transfer the money to an account I've set up and I'll buy it for you." Thomas told Myron.

"But if you want me to buy it you'll better let me know soon." Thomas said.

"Ok." Myron agreed.

"Well I have to run." Thomas got up to leave.

"Thanks again for telling me about the deal."

"Don't mention it." Thomas said as he walked away.

The $100 000 Myron had mentioned he had "borrowed" from Tyrone. Myron had already transferred the money from Tyrone's, to his own private account.

He was thinking about if he should let Thomas invest the money for him or if he should turn to the stock broker.

"I'll sleep on it." Myron told himself.

On the way home from work that day he thought about what he was going to do with all of that money he was going to make.

Maybe he would even buy that boat he'd had his eyes on for some time.

When he came home and got inside of his house, Cassie his wife had cooked dinner and was setting the table.

"A former model and a great cook as well." Myron thought to himself.

Cassie noticed that Myron had come home.

"Hey honey." She said smiling at Myron.

"Hi." Myron stood there smiling and thinking about all the things he and Cassie could do with all of that money.

"You're very happy today." Cassie observed.

"Well I'm about to make a deal that's going to make us a lot of money." "Really, how much." She asked with obvious interest.

"Maybe even up to a million."

"A million dollars, are you serious." Cassie asked.

"Yes."

"And it's nothing Illegal?" She asked.

"No sweetheart It's totally safe." He told his wife with a lie.

Myron didn't want to tell Cassie about that he had "borrowed" the money he was going to invest from Tyrone.

"Well honey, what are we going to do with all of that money?" She had a big smile on her face.

"I'm sure we'll think of something."

They kissed for a bit before they had dinner. After dinner and some TV they went to bed.

Myron got into bed and then a moment later his wife came into the bedroom wearing a sexy lingerie.

"Wow honey you look great." Myron was rising to the occasion.

"Well I thought the soon to be a millionaire would like this outfit." He got a hard on seeing his wife in that outfit.

Cassie proceeded to walk over to bed and got on top of Myron. They started kissing a bit. He started to remove his underwear revealing his hard 6 inch dick. Cassie then stood up on the bed and removed her panties looking down at him.

She then sat down on Myron's stomach, rubbing her ass against his dick.

"Ahh yeah." He was grunting.

"You like that uh." Cassie said in her sexy voice.

"Ahhhh." Myron let out another grunt as he came.

He spurted his load on Cassie's ass and her back.

"Oh Myron, not again! I was looking forward to a real nice time." "I'm sorry honey." He replied. This wasn't the first time Myron had cum before they had even begun making love. And even if he could hold it he would only last for no more than 5 minutes.

Un-be-known to Myron, Cassie had actually bought a few dildos because of this.

"We could wait awhile and then I'm sure I will be able to do it." Myron said.

"Don't bother." Said Cassie sounding a bit pissed and soon went to sleep.

The next day, Myron decided to contact the stock broker that Thomas had told him about and tell him to buy the stocks for him.

Myron called the stock broker and they talked for a bit. Strangely Myron thought he recognized the voice on the phone but at the time he thought nothing of it.

"And how many stocks do you want to buy." The stock broker asked.

"As many as I can get for $100 000." Myron told him.

"Ok, you have my account number so just have your bank transfer the sum and you'll have the stock documents tomorrow." He told Myron.

"Ok." Said Myron and hung up the phone.

Myron called his bank and told them to transfer the money to the stock brokers account.

"Soon I'll be rich." Myron thought to himself with a smile on his face.

Two days past and Myron had not received any stock documents yet.

He decided to call the stock broker and ask him about it.

When he called the number there was no answer. Myron tried a few more times that day, but there was no answer.

The next day he tried some more but now there was an automated voice from the phone company, telling him that there were no subscriber to the number he had called.

By now he had begun to feel a bit concerned. So he decided to talk to Thomas.

Myron went over to the place where they usually met but there was no sign of Thomas anywhere. He then called Thomas number, and as with the stock brokers number, there was a voice telling him that there was no subscriber to the number he had dialed.

Then it hit him.

He had been ripped off. The stock broker's voice that he had recognized was Thomas.

Myron's first thought was to call the police, but then he remembered that it wasn't even his money, it was Tyrone's.

"My god, what am I going to tell Tyrone?" He thought to himself. He actually began to feel a bit scared about what Tyrone might do to him.

During the weekend all Myron could think about was how he could get out of this mess, but he couldn't come up with anything. Cassie had asked him why he looked so down. He couldn't tell her the real reason so he just made up some work related stuff.

But then Monday came and he was on his way to Tyrone. "Maybe he won't notice that there is some money missing." He thought to himself.

The elevator stopped and Myron got out and walked over to Tyrone's apartment. He knocked and then went inside.

"Hi Myron, you got some papers for me?"

"Yes, here you go."

"Give them to Jermaine." Tyrone ordered.

Myron handed the papers to Tyrone's personal manager Jermaine, he always read them before Tyrone signed them.

In the apartment there sat two of Tyrone's friends as well.

"So everything is ok at the office?" Tyrone asked.

"Ye... Yes." Myron answered nervously.

"Well the reason that I ask is because I had an accountant go over all my accounts to see if everything was ok." Tyrone went on.

Myron now started to sweat even more.

"Are you sweating Myron?"

"Well it's just a bit warm in here, that's all."

"You know Myron, the accountant found that there was some money missing from one of my accounts. $100 000 dollars to be exact."

"I...I." Myron tried to say something.

"And do you know what else Myron?"

"N...n...no." Myron stammered.

"The money was transferred to your private account Myron." The Tank looked rather pissed.

"But my accountant says that the money is not there anymore, where is It?"

"I...I...I lost it." Myron said looking down at his shoes.

"First you steal $100 000 of my money then you lose it?"

"I'm...I'm so sorry."

"You know what happens to people who try to steal from me?" Tyrone Asked.

By now Tyrone's two friends had gotten up and was standing behind Myron.

"Yes." Myron answered in a scared voice. He remembered what Tyrone had done to a guy that stole a couple of thousand from him.

After Tyrone was through with him, the guy was forced to lie in the hospital for a month and after which he couldn't walk right. All that just because he had stolen a couple of thousand. And Myron had lost $100 000 of Tyrone's money.

"But because you have made me a couple of millions in the past, I'm going to go easy on you."

"Thank you Tyrone."

"I will allow you to return to your job working for me, I will even give you $20 000 dollars." Tyrone said.

"Because in a month I want that money to be $200 000 dollars." If the money I gave you haven't turned into $200 000 in a month I will be forced to do something very bad to you. Do you understand Myron?"

"Y...Yes."

"There's one more thing I want from you Myron."

"What's...that?"

"I want your wife Cassie for a week."

Myron's eyes flew open. "What!" Myron said as he got a punch in the stomach from one of Tyrone's friends. "Lower your voice." One of them told Myron.

"I want Cassie to come and stay with me here for a week." Tyrone said. "Either this or, well you know what would happen to you."

"But...but she's my wife." Myron almost started to cry.

"Well you should have thought of that before you stole from me. Now I want you to bring her here tomorrow. Is that clear?"

"But she might not want to."

"Then it's your job to persuade her. Just have her here tomorrow." Tyrone ordered.

"O...ok." Myron finally agreed.

"Ok then, will you help Myron to the elevator?" Tyrone asked his friends.

They each grabbed one of Myron's arms and then dragged him out and into the elevator.

On the way home from Tyrone's Myron sat in his car almost crying. Myron didn't want to bring his wife to Tyrone but he couldn't see any other way.

When he got home that day he went inside and explained everything to Cassie. "What? He wants me to stay with him for a week!" Cassie yelled.

"I really don't want you to do it but there's no other way. It might not be so bad, and it's only for a week. If you don't, well I told you what he did to that other guy that stole from him."

"I know, and I don't want you to get hurt but couldn't we go to the police?" Cassie asked.

"No we can't, you know it wasn't my money that I lost."

"Well how could you be so stupid as to steal from this guy?" She was totally pissed off.

"I'm sorry honey, I just wanted to get some fast money."

"Does he expect me to sleep with him as well?" Cassie asked.

Myron looked down at his shoes. "He might."

They talked and argued for a couple of hours more, then they went to bed, but they could not sleep much. They had decided that Cassie would spend the week with Tyrone. The afternoon the next day Cassie packed some things and then they were off to Tyrone's penthouse.

As they stepped out of the elevator on the top floor Myron looked over at his wife. "Are you sure about this Cassie?" He asked.

"If it will prevent you from getting hurt."

They knocked on the door to Tyrone's apartment and gave each other a little kiss before they went inside.

"Well Myron so good of you to come." "And Cassie you look hot as usual." Tyrone shook Cassie's hand. Cassie looked down and saw her small hand engulfed by Tyrone's huge, black hand.

"Hi." Cassie said.

Myron didn't like the way Tyrone looked at Cassie but he knew that he didn't have a choice.

"You didn't have to bring your own clothes, I have bought some clothes for you to wear." Tyrone explained.

"Well Myron, you can pick her up in a week, but you'll still see her here a couple of times this week when you bring over my papers to sign. You can leave now, I'll take good care of your wife."

"But..." Myron tried to say something.

"No buts, do you want to leave by yourself or do you want the guys to throw you out in front of your wife?"

"Ok, I'll leave."

"Bye honey." Cassie spoke up in a sad voice.

"Bye." He left the apartment. On the way home, he felt humiliated, having to hand over his wife to Tyrone.

"Well Cassie how about you strip for us?" Tyrone was grinning.

"What, I can't strip in front of all of you."

"Well guys, I'll better ease her into this in the bedroom alone this time." Tyrone told his two friends.

Cassie began to feel more and more nervous. "Was he actually going to make her strip in front of him?" Cassie wondered to herself as Tyrone grabbed her hand and took her into the bedroom, closing the door.

When they got into the bedroom Tyrone got up close to Cassie and placed his hands on her hips.

"You know Cassie, you really are a very sexy woman."

He then began to kiss her neck, moving his kisses up towards her mouth. When he got up to her mouth Cassie didn't open her mouth to Tyrone's kisses.

"Open your mouth." Cassie slowly opened her mouth as Tyrone slid his tongue inside her mouth. "I'm doing this for Myron." Cassie thought to herself. By now Tyrone had his hands on Cassie's ass and were squeezing them as he was tongue kissing her.

Cassie actually began to feel a bit horny by all of this. She felt ashamed to be having these feelings with another man other than her husband Myron.

"Now let's take these clothes off."

He then removed his own shirt and pants leaving only his boxers on.

Cassie looked at Tyrone as he was undressing. "He really does have a great body." She thought to herself.

"Well take your blouse and skirt off." He demanded.

Cassie began to remove her clothing. She was wearing a pair of white panties and a matching bra.

"Damn you look good." Tyrone said as he went up to Cassie.

He started kissing her and he now had his hand on her breasts. Cassie felt something hard pressing against her stomach.

"Oh god that can't be his..." She thought to herself.

Tyrone had now unsnapped her bra and threw it on the floor. He went down and started sucking on her hard nipples.

"Mmm." She let out a moan. "Oh my god, did I just moan." Cassie wondered.

"You like that huh?"

Cassie's face turned red. "No I just..." She tried to say that she didn't. "Well I love to suck on your small white tits." Then Tyrone started kissing her breasts again but this time he was moving down toward her panties. When he got down to them he grabbed them and slid them down her legs.

He then touched her now fully exposed pussy lips. "You're quite wet down here, aren't you?" Tyrone observed as he quickly licked her pussy.

"Oh god, that feels so good." Cassie thought to herself.

Tyrone licked her for a minute more then he stood up.

"Well it's time for you to get down on your knees." He wanted her to take out his cock.

Cassie slowly got down on her knees and now had her face right in front of his boxers. She could see the outline of something huge.

"Pull them down."

Cassie slowly reached over and pulled his boxers down. Her eyes then opened up wide.

"Oh god." She said out loud.

"That's something else than your husbands isn't it." Tyrone asked.

"It sure is." She said still looking at it. It must have been 11 inches long and very thick as well.

"So you never had a black man before?" Tyrone asked.

"No never."

"Well now you know what you have been missing."

"I sure do." She agreed.

She then reached up and slowly grabbed it. Cassie couldn't get her hand around it, it was too thick.

"Now suck it bitch."

Cassie felt even more ashamed now than before, because she really wanted to suck that black cock. She opened her mouth and got his big cockhead inside. She started sucking on it.

"That's a good slut."

By now she was really slurping on it.

Cassie thought that it was great having this huge cock inside of her mouth.

"Tell me you like it bitch."

The dirtier he talked to her the more she got turned on.

"Oh yes I love your big black cock."

A moment later he pulled her up and carried her over to the bed and laid her down on it.

Tyrone then got on top of her, getting in between her now spread legs. "I'm gonna fuck the shit out of you."

By this time Cassie had forgotten all about Myron and all she wanted now was to get fucked.

"Oh yes, fuck me with that big cock of yours."

Tyrone took a hold of his cock and placed it up against her pussy. And then a second later he just shoved it in.

"Oh goddddd." Cassie screamed out.

"Yeah bitch." Tyrone said as he began to fuck her.

He was slamming his black cock in and out of her. It was a hot scene, this huge black man on top of this white woman.

"Oh yes oh yes, I cumming." Cassie couldn't believe it, she had never had an orgasm before when a guy had fucked her. A few minutes later Tyrone flipped Cassie around and got up behind her. He then shoved his cock into her pussy from behind. She was moaning like hell.

Tyrone was pumping her pussy hard. Then a moment later he pulled out.

"Get up here bitch."

Cassie turned around and got her face up to Tyrone's cock. He was pulling on it in front of her face.

"Open your mouth." He grunted.

A second later Tyrone shot his load. He spurted wad after wad of cum right in her face. He got his cock down close to her open mouth and she took a lot of sperm right inside her mouth. Cassie swallowed all she could. She had never had cum in her mouth before much less swallowed it.

Tyrone soon stopped cumming. She took his cockhead into her mouth and sucked it clean.

"That's a good slut. You liked that didn't you?" Tyrone asked.

"Oh yes, I never thought cum could taste so good."

That night all Tyrone and Cassie did was fuck.

Myron on the other hand laid home in bed thinking about his sweet wife. "She probably wouldn't allow Tyrone to sleep with her." Myron thought to himself as he went to sleep.

Two days had past and Myron was driving over to Tyrone's to give him some more papers to sign.

He took the elevator up and knocked on the door as usual. He looked around the apartment, but there was no sign of Cassie or Tyrone.

"Myron, you have some papers for Tyrone?" Jermaine asked.

"Yes, here." He handed them over to Jermaine.

"Have a seat while we wait for Tyrone."

Myron sat down and soon he began to hear some noises coming from Tyrone's bedroom. It actually sounded like people moaning.

"That couldn't be Cassie." Myron thought to himself. Myron looked over at Tyrone's two friends who sat in the next couch. They were grinning at him. Then Myron heard a female voice scream. "It sounded like she screamed oh my god or something like that." Myron thought to himself.

5 minutes later the door to the bedroom opened and Tyrone came out wearing a robe. "Well hi Myron."

"Hello."

"These papers are ready for you to sign." Jermaine told Tyrone.

"Ok."

"Well Myron that wife of yours is one hot slut. She just can't get enough of black cock now that she has had a taste." Tyrone told Myron.

Myron felt humiliated by what Tyrone said but he didn't know what to say. He now knew that it was Cassie in the bedroom and that she had just fucked Tyrone.

Tyrone signed the papers.

Myron then heard someone walking in Tyrone's bedroom and he turned around to see who it was.

He only saw a glimpse of a naked woman walking in the bedroom and then he heard her say something. "I'm just going to take a shower."

Myron recognized the voice. It was Cassie. "Well that was the last paper, so you can go now." Tyrone told Myron. He got up and walked over to the door. And just as he opened the door he heard Tyrone say something to one of his black friends.

"Why don't you go and help Cassie in the shower." Tyrone told his friend.

"Glad to."

On the way home Myron thought about what had happened. Not only had Cassie been fucking Tyrone, she had most likely been sleeping with all of them.

It went two more days and Myron had to go to Tyrone's again. This time when Myron came up to his apartment Tyrone was sitting on a couch in the room.

"Hi Myron."

"Hi."

"Here's the papers." Myron said as he gave them to Jermaine.

"Well sit down."

Myron sat. "Hi Cassie, why don't you come over and sit down." Tyrone told Cassie as she came into the room.

She walked over and sat down next to Tyrone.

Myron's eyes flew open when he saw what she was wearing.

She was wearing a very skimpy bikini. A small light green top and a matching thong. Cassie smiled as she gave Tyrone a kiss.

"Hi Myron." She greeted him.

"Are you ok?" Myron asked.

"I'm just terrific." She said smiling.

"I just can't believe this ex model married a wimp like you Myron." Myron said nothing.

"Just look at her body, these sweet legs and these firm tits." Tyrone said as he squeezed Cassie's breasts.

Myron's face turned red with jealousy.

"And not to mention her tight pussy." Tyrone said as he slid his hand down inside of her bikini thong.

Myron looked at Cassie as she started to moan.

"But you know what she does best Myron?"

Myron didn't respond. "Well why don't you show him Cassie."

"Ok." She had a big smile on her face. She reached over and unzipped Tyrone's pants and then pulled out his huge black cock.

Myron couldn't help but to look at his wife as she got her lips around his cock and started sucking. Myron felt so humiliated, this was a woman he loved who was sucking on this black man's cock. Myron was just about ready to leave. He started to get up when he was pushed down on the couch. It was one of Tyrone's friends who stood behind him.

"You're not leaving just yet, are you?" Tyrone asked. "Ahh, she can really suck cock."

She was bobbing her head up and down on Tyrone's cock. She was making these loud slurping sounds. "Tell your husband what you love to do Cassie." "I just love to suck big black dick."

Tyrone then laid his hand on Cassie's head. "Ahh yes." He started to grunt.

Tyrone was cumming. Myron could see some white liquid coming out of Cassie's mouth as she sucked on his massive member.

"Ah god, you are a good slut." Tyrone groaned.

"Thank you." She replied.

Myron couldn't believe his eyes. His wife Cassie had let this man cum right into her mouth and she actually appeared to have enjoyed it.

"Why don't you give your husband a kiss before you wash up Cassie?" She walked over to Myron and gave him a big, long kiss on his mouth. Myron was shocked at what she had just done.

She then went into the bathroom and washed up. She then walked out of the apartment.

"Have fun in the pool." Tyrone said.

"I will."

"Well here's your papers, you can leave now Myron."

As Myron walked towards the elevator he looked into the pool room through the glass windows, and there he saw Cassie in a small pool along with two other black guys. And she had already removed her bikini top.

Later when Myron was driving home, all he could think about was Cassie. How could she sleep with all of those guys? And even worse, she appeared to like it as well.

For the next couple of days Myron wondered about all the things that Cassie was doing at Tyrone's.

It had now gone a week since he dropped her off at his place. And today was the day that Myron was driving over to Tyrone's to pick her up. When Myron got up to Tyrone's penthouse, he knocked on the door and went inside. And there in the middle of the room stood Tyrone, Jermaine and his two friends and they were all naked.

Cassie was also there, but she was dressed and she was giving all of them a long kiss good-bye. "Hi honey, I'll be right out." Cassie said.

"Ok, I'll take your bag."

A few minutes later Cassie was on her way out.

"Well we'll see you on Thursday Cassie." Tyrone said.

"I'll be here."

In the elevator, Myron asked her what he had meant.

"Well honey, Tyrone is having a small party on Thursday and he's invited me to come."

"You're not going are you?"

"Of course I am."

"But you don't have to, he has had you for a week and now you don't have to be with him anymore."

"Well honey, sometimes I just need to have a real man take me." Cassie Explained.

"But."

"No buts, from now on I'll be going over to Tyrone's a couple of times a week."

Myron just looked down and reluctantly nodded ok.

"And you know what, I think he's going to take me up the ass the next time." Cassie told Myron with a smile on her face.

A week later Myron happened to see Tyrone talking to Thomas. The guy who had ripped him off.

And the same week Myron found out that Tyrone had hired Thomas to get him to steal and invest in that fake company, so that Tyrone could have his way with Cassie. It was at that point that Myron began to plan how to murder The Tank and Thomas.

Be Careful What You Ask For

Todd's such a jerk; sometimes I don't know why I stay with him. We dated for two years before marrying almost 8 years ago. You know the old saying, 'Familiarity breeds contempt,' well, that really holds true for our relationship. The stupid stuff he does would make just about any woman want a divorce I think.

His latest thing has been to get me into bed with his buddy from work. I mean can you believe that? What a jerk!

He brought the subject up last week after taking me out to Applebee's for dinner. We were sitting in the restaurant just finishing when he looks over at me and says, "Merrell, what do you think of Marco?"

I had no idea what he meant. I just looked at him questioningly.

He continued with, "You know, do you think he's a sexy looking guy?"

To be truthful I did think he was sexy. Marco is about 6-feet-5 and has almost jet-black skin and muscular shoulders with a really trim waist. Unlike Todd he's well built and takes great care of his body. But that wasn't the point, why did Todd want to know if I thought he was sexy? I kept looking at him without saying anything. I wanted to see where he was going with this.

"Look Merrell, I've been thinking that maybe you're not all that happy in bed any more. I was just talking to Marco today at work and mentioned that we hadn't done "it" for almost three weeks. And he started giving me this ration of shit that 'if he were your husband he'd keep you so satisfied in bed that you'd be coming to him and begging for it."

I kept quiet and just stared at him like he was a bug or something. But my cold response didn't stop him from continuing. "Well, when he said that it made me think. I, err. I got this idea that I wanted to share with you. You know, to see what you thought. Anyway, I was wondering if you ever thought about Marco, you know, sexually?"

I couldn't help myself, "What do you mean Todd?" I just had to ask the question.

He looked really nervous, "I, uh. I was just wondering if you might be interested in messing around with Marco. You know, maybe a threesome or something?"

I couldn't believe my ears at first but from the stupid look on Todd's face I soon realized that he was serious. The stupid son of a bitch wanted me to fuck his friend so he could watch us. Un-fucking-believable!

***

We didn't talk all the way home. I had nothing to say to Todd and I think he was worried that he'd exposed his perverted mind to me once too often. But when we got home, guess what? Marco was there waiting in his car in our driveway. I was actually shocked! I was pissed, what a nerve. Did they think I'd just say, "Okay guys lets do it? C'mon in and lets screw!" What a fucking nerve they had.

Todd pulled up into the driveway and I got out slamming the car door and I stomped by Marco into the house. I was beyond pissed at that point.

To my surprise Marco and Todd came in after me. I'd thought that I had made my feelings known, but apparently not. I guess Todd must have an I Q of about 30. After some time, I came out of the bathroom to find Marco and Todd drinking beer in the living room. For some reason this made me angrier, what were they doing in there? Trying to work up another scheme to get me into bed? At that moment, they should have been thanking God that I didn't have access to an A K 47.

I had a sudden irrational thought. 'If Todd wanted me to fuck another man, maybe I should just go ahead and do it.' I'd been faithful to him for the ten years I'd known him, and believe me -- when I say that I've had plenty of opportunities to stray elsewhere.

As I stood in the hallway looking in on the two men I found myself wondering what it would be like to actually "be" with a black man. And the fact that Marco was a bit of a stud muffin didn't hurt. I suddenly realized that I was aroused by the possibility of being taken by that big, black beast with the rippling muscles. He definitely was a far cry from my flabby, out of shape husband.

With a sense of excitement I hurried back to our bedroom and quickly stripped off my outer clothing, leaving only my black-lace bra and panties. Then without thinking further about the consequences of my actions I called out, "Marco, would you come here for a minute?"

I waited with my heart in my throat listening to his footsteps on the creaky floorboards as he made his way down the hall to me. I have to admit, I was amused by the startled look on his face as he rounded the edge of the doorframe and saw that I was only in my underwear. He looked almost frightened for a moment.

Then I said, "Marco, my husband tells me that you'd like to screw me, is that true?" I was trying to shock him. But to my surprise he wasn't shocked, in fact he just gave me a big slow grin and said, "That would be my pleasure ma'am, and I think yours too." (At least the thug had something approaching good manners).

He didn't even hesitate, he just walked into the room like the dominant man he was and reached out and squeezed my boobs in his strong black hands. Then before I knew what was happening he gently pulled my bra away and scrunched down and began to suck on one nipple, while at the same time I felt a hand needing my ass-cheeks.

I "almost" couldn't believe that I was doing this, what was I thinking letting a complete stranger maul me like this. I didn't really know anything about Marco other than the few times I'd seen him at one or other of my husband's company functions.

Just as I was about to pull away from his grip and tell him to leave, Todd came in. He stood their sporting a big bulge in his LL Beans and I could tell that he was aroused. I looked at him as I stood there being sucked on and handled by his black friend. I looked at my husband and said, "Well asshole, you said you wanted this to happen, I hope you enjoy the fucking show." I quickly grabbed Marco's head and pulled him up to me and gave him a deep tongue-filled kiss.

I was surprised by his reaction, almost frightened by it in fact. As our lips met and my tongue slid past his full lips he suddenly became like an animal, I even heard him growl and grunt as he held me so close to his chest that I could barely breathe. He was all over me; his hands and fingers were playing over my flesh like a pianist.

Then I was on my back on our bed and Marco was tugging my panties off. I had no time to think, or to protest for that matter. He buried his face between my legs and started a rhythmic pleasuring of my pussy and clit that I'd never experienced before. He was good, really good.

Soon I was lost in the wonderful arousal he'd caused and was almost out of control. Marco had brought my animal lust out so fast that I was somewhat in a daze. I think at that moment I'd have done just about anything to get off, he'd made me so fucking horny.

This was so different from anything I'd ever experienced with Todd, or even the few guys I'd been with before him. Marco was a born lover and his smooth skin was a pleasure to touch. I think at that moment I loved Marco.

Then he was climbing up my body, positioning himself between my legs. I glanced down and saw his big black snaking toward me, all shiny and manly and I wanted nothing more than to be used by him, to become his helpless fuck-slave, to let him do anything he wanted to me. God, this sexy black man turned me on so much.

Even the thought of his shiny black skin next to mine set me on fire; I wanted him to rub himself against me, and to rub himself 'inside' me. To fuck my brains out! And sure enough, he plunged in with total confidence and began to thrust into me in a quick, competent manner that made my toes curl.

I had a crazy thought, for a moment I wondered if a black men's come would be white, but of course I knew that it would. It's just that I'd had no experience with black men before and never thought that I'd be under one servicing him like a willing whore. Marco's willing whore, it made me crazy with need just thinking those thoughts and I grabbed his shoulders and began thrusting back at him like a mad woman. I even Cried out, "Fuck me like a slut!"

I was soon breathless. Marco was humping away in me like an athlete, never missing his stride, it was wonderful to feel his strong swollen dick thrusting into me, to know that he was close to heaving his load deep into me. Just the thought of his sticky white come gushing into me brought on a wonderfully intense orgasm.

My body tensed and the lights seemed to go out as intense pleasure rushed through every pour of my body. I shivered and groaned as wave after wave of intense ecstasy shot through every nerve ending.

And all the while my big black sex machine, thrust in and out, in and out. It was fucking fantastic; he was like a god to me just then. I began to moan and squirm around under this thrusting body, I realized somewhere in the back of my mind that if Marco kept this up much longer I was going to pass out.

Then at the last moment before I began to slip into oblivion, I felt my handsome lover stiffen and my body was smashed into the mattress as he made one final, mighty thrust, pinning me to the bed. I could actually feel him blast my insides with his hot come. It was a wonderful moment that tiny spurting feeling deep inside, I knew what he was doing and it made me come again. I clung to his sweaty body as I rushed head long into another bout of hot mad ecstasy.

It took us a full 5 minutes I think, before we could disengage our bodies enough to come back into the real world. That's when I noticed Todd still standing there. He'd moved up over us and had jacked off onto us while we were lost in our world of pleasure. I noticed that he'd sprayed his come all over Marco's back. I think Marco wasn't real happy about that.

But then I resolved to make Marco as happy as I could from now on. And frankly I didn't care if Todd jacked his brains out. As far as I was concerned I was done wasting my time on that total wimp. I decided that Marco would be a very long adventure to be enjoyed whenever and wherever possible. I made sure I got Marco's phone number before he left our pad. After he left, I went up to my perverted idiot, Todd and gave him a solid slap across his face. "Guess what Todd? That huge black mother fucker is going to be visiting us a whole lot from now on and don't you ever spray your filthy spunk on him again, you got it buster?"

Black Police Predators
Part 1

It was a beautiful summer night. Their hair was blowing in the wind. Hank had the top down to the convertible, country music blasting, and Stacey lounging across the big seat, her head on Hank's lap while her bare feet dangling out the passenger side. They had left Talledega just after the race, fought the traffic to get clear, and now were heading on the home stretch. Well, going down route 29 through Alabama isn't exactly a "home stretch", but it beats going through Montgomery, and besides, cutting the back roads was routine for them in the day time.

It was just after 9pm, in the dark of night, when the headlights popped on, and then the flashing lights followed.

"Damn, where did he come from" Hank exclaimed.

"What's that?" asked Stacey.

"A freakn' cop.....that's what!" Hank replied somewhat pissed.

They slowed down, and Stacey got in the upright position.

"License and registration please" asked the cop. He was shining the light straight in their faces, blinding both of them.

"What's wrong" Hank asked.

"Sixty three in a Fifty....that's what" replied the cop. Then a second voice appeared from the other side. He too turned on his light, pointing at Stacey's white and red legs then over to Hank's.

"No seatbelts either, another violation" he added.

"Ah guys, this car was built in 1960...they didn't have seatbelts then, nor any seatbelt laws then" Hank interjected.

"What are you...a lawyer or something?" Asked the cop.

"No...but this car is registered as a classic...and part of the true restoration is to have it all original, thus, no seatbelts." Hank added.

After looking over the registration, the cop commanded "let's have a look in the trunk, if you don't mind."

"What for?" Hank asked. "We just came from Talledega and all we have is our suitcase from staying overnight."

"Well, if you have nothing to hide, I'm sure it won't be a problem then...will it" snapped the officer. "You know, I can get a search warrant....as late as it is, the Judge will be pissed, but that's up to you." The cop replied.

"Oh...alright" and Hank got out, and walked to the back of the car. The second officer instructed Stacey to just sit there, and went back with his partner. Hank opened up the trunk, and looked inside to see his suitcase, which seemed to be dwarfed by the huge trunk his car had.

"See, that's all I have." Hank snapped.

It was so dark on this Alabama night, you couldn't see your hand in front of your face...and the cops knew it too. As the light was shined on the suitcase, the second officer unzipped it, and proceeded to look inside. Not knowing.....Hank didn't see the two tiny bags of cocaine under the officers thumbs, cocked under in his palm. As the cop pulled his hand out....

"Well, well, well. What do we have here" he exclaimed, as he pulled the two tiny packets out. "A little fun package here?" he added.

"I have no idea. I know they're NOT mine" Hank said, excited...eyes wide as saucers. He knew they weren't his or Stacey's, but sensed they were in deep shit, and knew they were set up.

"Put your hands behind you" the first cop said as Hank was whisked around. "You're under arrest for having a foreign substance, possible drugs."

"What...you've got to be kidding?" He said as he was handcuffed.

The second officer retrieved Stacey out of the front seat, and handcuffed her too. She was shocked and crying with all the confusion going on, and admits of pleas and begging, nothing stopped them from being arrested.

They both had canvas bags put over their heads, which both Hank and Stacey thought was odd...and as they sat in the back seat of the cruiser, began to chat back and forth. The officer jammed on the brakes, and hollered "cut the damn yakking out, hear me. There'll be no talking....nothing, understand" They both replied, and silence was all they heard.

The car weaved, bounced and swerved… hit holes and what else could be felt on the ride to the station.... (or were they....Hank sensed something wrong here).

After the car stopped, Hank was taken in first, then Stacey. Hank was ushered into a cell. His jail cell door was shut, and after poking his hands back out, like instructed, the cuffs were removed. He immediately removed the canvas bag and looked around. Everything looked like a jail. There was a toilet, sink, 19 inch TV and a single bed. Everything Hank ever saw on TV shows. Then he looked around. The jail cell looked like a small town type, kind of like "Mayberry". Just a desk, phone, light, and this huge black cop just standing there.....but with a modern day "Lone Ranger" mask on in two colors ,black and white.

"Hey...what's this?" Hank asked. NO answer given, the officer just sat down. Anything Hank asked.......nothing....not a peep.

Stacey was moved into what seemed a house. When inside, her bag was taken off, and cuffs as well.

"What gives...this isn't a jail" she said, as she looked at the huge black officer wearing the exact same kind of mask. "And what's with the mask...hey....you're not a cop!"

"Well, I am...these mask are used to hide our real identity. We're in undercover work as well, and can't afford anyone to know who we really are." He boldly replied.

"This is the jail keeper's house. You'll stay here until we can sort this stuff out." The officer continued. Stacey looked around. Everything was neat and orderly, bright colors everywhere. It had a big living room with adjoining dining room and big open kitchen...all within eyesight. Very nice furniture as well. One thing...bars on the windows. "Why the bars?" she asked. "Like I said, until we sort this out, this is where you'll stay, while your husband is rotting in the jail."

"Well, first we'll do a check on the car. Then after throwing in "no seatbelts", along with speeding, and now drugs, either one or both of you will be facing at least ten years for transporting illegal drugs." the officer said rather harshly.

"Oh my God!" Was all Stacy could muster, as she started crying...putting her hands over her face? "It's not ours...test us...we're clean...but it's NOT ours...I have NO idea how it got there...honest!" She rambled on.

The officer knew she was weak, and didn't waste any time in turning things to HIS way of thinking.

"Well, things have ways of working themselves out." He said, smiling.

"I hope so. It's not ours, I mean that...please officer, please believe me!" Stacey started pleading, still crying. The officer went into the other room, and brought back a box of Kleenex, took out one and handed it to her. Stacey began to wipe her eyes, still sobbing uncontrollably.

"Listen...like I said....things can work themselves out, if you know what I mean." He said again, as he put his arm around Stacey and sat her down on the couch.

"What do you mean?" Stacey asked, looking up at him. Her 5' 4" frame seemed so small to his. She guessed he stood just over 6 feet and huge… maybe 220 pounds or so.

"Well, in life, we all make deals. Do this for that...you know, kind of like the barter system" He explained, as he cupped his other hand on her nice firm thigh.

"What...are you crazy?" She shouted, pushing herself away from the cop.

He just got up and went over to the phone... picked it up and said, "get him ready for the ride to the State Penn...we'll worry about the Judge later." He calmly said.

"You can't do that! It's against the law! We're entitled to legal counsel and to see the Judge." she said crying more and more now.

The big black cop went over to Stacey, grabbed her by both arms and picked her completely off the floor...her barely 105 pound body fell limp. "I AM the law here lady. Do you understand that? I am the law, and don't you forget that."

"Alright, alright.....please...don't send my husband away...please. I'll do anything." She said, giving in...sobbing.

"Anything?" He asked in a commanding tone.

"Anything....just don't hurt me." Stacey said softly. Stacey searched her inner thoughts. She had always been faithful to Hank, and now, she thought, he needed me more than ever. She'd do anything to keep him outta jail and so long as Hank didn't know....she'd think up something later to tell him.

The big black cop moved closer. "I knew you'd look at it my way" as he again sat her down on the couch. This time, he put a big kiss on her lips, probing his tongue deep inside. While doing so, he then started to cup her breast, feeling how round, soft they were and yet firm the nipple was and then slid his hand over to the other one. That one too was firm. Can it be that she liked his manner??? Inside Stacey's' mind, she tried to block out that he was black, and keeping her eyes shut tight. After a few minutes of him massaging her tits and him being so soft and gentle, she started to like it. 'My God... I can't be liking this' she thought. But she was, her emotions were getting confused with this all new feeling...not only a different man...but a black one at that. He moved to kissing her neck, just pecking softly, as his hand began the task of unbuttoning her flowered purple blouse, and when he was finished he cupped his hand to a lovely, laced bra that barely held in her breast. 'What is this...damn...I can't be liking this' she kept saying to herself. 'It feels so good' she kept saying over and over again...as she felt the soft, smooth stroking of his fingertips tracing her bra line, and then over to her nipple. His breath was picking up as he went lower and lower down her sternum, to the cleavage of her breast. He traced his tongue across the top of her low cut bra, and poked it inside, touching the very edge of her nipple. By now, Stacey had picked up her arm instinctively and put it on the back of the officer's shaven head. She gave no resistance when he slid his hand around to her back to unsnap her bra, and free her breast. 'What am I doing...I can't believe this, but, it feels so good...and ...he's not hurting me' she thought. Her emotions were surely confused by now. After he unsnapped the bra, he took his fingertip, just one of them, and ever so lightly traced a path from her back, around the side, to the nipple. She jumped...and he sensed she was liking this, and he'd only begun. He took her nipple in between his forefinger and thumb and began a soft twisting, then held it as he rotated it in circle with her whole breast. Once in a while… he'd give a sharp squeeze, and then start all over again, finishing by taking his tongue and licking the very end of her nipple. Shots of sparks were shooting through Stacey's' body. She'd never experienced this before... this was all new. Oh, Hank and her have had great sex before, but Hank never sent sparks through her. Who was this man....what was he doing to her, she kept thinking, her mind swirling round and around. He stood up, and offering his hand, Stacey put hers in his and stood up. Not saying a word, he then proceeded to slide her blouse off, followed by her bra.

"Yes...very lovely...very lovely indeed." He whispered as he now took both hands to both breast and repeated the aforementioned rhythm.

Stacey put her hands on his hips, trying to stay calm...but her breathing gave her away. He then knew she was enjoying it. Next, he moved his hands down to her belt...unbuckled it, unbuttoned her shorts, unzipped them and pushed them over her hips, dropping them to the floor as well. 'I'm standing in front of this stranger, who's Black, with my nipples erect as hell and just my panties on....and it's exciting me....why's that?' Stacey kept asking herself. The Black Cop, towering over her like a pole, bent over, and placed his lips on her breast...and began to suck one...then moved over to the other. Every once in a while....he'd slightly nibble on her pert nipples, and finish off by swirling his tongue around her tits. 'God...what he does to me, I can't be enjoying this...but I am....dear Lord...I am' she kept saying to herself. As he was sucking those wonderful tits of hers, he moved his hand down over her nice milky white ass, over top of those smooth panties, and came across the front...and cupped his hand solidly on her pussy. Stacey gave no resistance...as a matter of fact, she opened her legs a tad for him to gain entrance. When she did this, there was no hiding her emotions at this point...for by now, her pussy was warm to the touch and very, very wet.

"What do we have here? You're really enjoying this...aren't you?" Stacey, still saying nothing, was now holding onto the back of his shaven head and his muscular arm...that was stroking her ever increasingly eager pussy. The cop slowly dropped to his knees, and began kissing lower and lower on her stomach to the top of her skimpy panty line. By inserting his thumbs on either side of her panty, he easily removed them. With one constant slide to the floor, Stacey just stepped out of them.

"Look at what we have here....and slightly shaven at that." He laughed. It was true, Stacey always clipped the hairs on her pussy during the summer, so as they wouldn't stick outside of her bathing suit. He began to flicker his tongue on the very top of her cunt....poking deeper and deeper. 'Damn....I can't take this much longer....what is he doing to me....his tongue...his tongue...how good he uses it' she thought to herself. 'What am I saying...' she thought. She finally opened her eyes and looked down. She could see this Black shaven head with this pink tongue darting in between her legs, sending her higher and higher through the roof with lust.

"That is one fine pussy, you're gonna love giving it up to this Black Man, lady." He quipped as he began to take off his shirt, and then his pants. Stacey just stood there, looking over this huge statue of a man. He had huge shoulders with a large neck, big bi-ceps, a six pack ab section and muscular legs. But what got Stacey's attention the most, was the large mound in his briefs. 'My God...it looks huge. That can't be all him' she thought. He grabbed her little white hand, and placed it on his red briefs.

"This will be the best cock you ever had."

Part 2

The Black cop was now starting to remove his red briefs. As they slid down, Stacey let go of the huge bulge that she had a hold of and was now transfixed of the size of his cock that sprang out. Even though it was only half erect, it was still bigger than her husband's dick.

"My God... you're so big. I don't know." Stacey mused as his dick sprang to total life.

"Don't know about what? That you can't, or you'd rather see your husband go to prison?" Quipped the cop.

With her eyes still transfixed on his cock, the cop again grabbed her little white hand, and placed it on his growing cock. Stacey felt how thick and dense it felt, as well as how heavy it felt.

"Over here, by the coffee table." Stacey moved over to the elegant table.

"Place your palms face down on the table, and open your legs Stacey." He told her. She did as instructed. He approached her from behind, and began the process of "teasing" her. He slid his now rock hard cock between her legs, and just slid it back and forth on her wet pussy. His head massaging her wet lips, letting her senses build. 'God knows I love my husband...but this guy is sending shocks through me like I've never had before...why am I starting to enjoy this...why?' She kept asking herself over and over. Even though her mind was totally confused by now...one side saying no, while the other saying yes, and by all means her body abandoning her, she was starting to enjoy the feel of this 'log' between her legs, and he wasn't even in her yet.

"I can't do this...please....don't hurt me...please." She again began, begging... sobbing at the same time.

"You might be saying no, but I can tell your pussy is saying yes by how wet my cock is, Stacey....and it's ready for it."

With that, he slowly just inserted the head of his cock, and let it rest there for a few seconds.

"Ah..." Stacey mumbled.

Not saying a word, the cop pulled it out and again slowly inserted the head back in, this time adding a couple of inches of the shaft as well.

"Umph...ah...oh... it hurts." Stacey whimpered.

And again, he let it rest there. "You'll get used to it....your pussy will adjust...and then you'll want more...trust me." He chuckled as he slowly resumed his exploration.

By now, with the soft touch of his large hands on her hips, he guided her hips back and forth on his cock, until a rhythm was established. After what seemed only a couple of minutes, Stacey's mind was beginning to really work overtime. 'The pains going away, and his cock...it's huge, it's really filling me up...what is this pleasure that this Black cock is giving me? Can it be?' she thought. Stacey kept her rhythm up, and not even realizing that he had taken his hands off her hips, was now doing it by herself. Spasms were jumping up and down her cunt muscles...building up to her first climax, and within only a few minutes she began to shutter to her first orgasm.

"See, I told ya. That pussy knows a real cock, and it wants more." Without even knowing it, Stacey was now bucking back and forth, taking on more and more of that Black dick, while he just stood there. It was so deep in her by now that not only was she fucking that cock, she'd ground her hips against his as well.

"That's it baby...fuck that cock. Let it rip!"

Within another few minutes, Stacey had another climax and was starting to build on her next one. 'What, oh my God...this feels so good...Hank never gave me cock like this. Hank, oh honey...I'm doing this for you...please forgive me. Ah!' She repeated over and over in her mind. After a few more climaxes, Stacey started to slow down a bit, but still not pulling away from that thick shaft that was giving her rush after rush.

"Ok, now I'M really going to fuck you." And with that, he began to slowly pound his huge cock deeper and deeper in Stacey. Holding onto her hips, he raised his strokes to a faster pace for the next few minutes, and then picked up the pace after that. He was slapping that cock so hard in her by now, you could hear his balls slapping against the top of her cunt every time he thrust his dick home.

"Oh yeah baby...take it....that's it, feel what a real cock is!" He kept saying. And even with that, he began to taunt her. "You like this black cock... don't you...huh...don't you?" he slapped her ass. When she didn't answer at first, he repeated it again.

"You like this cock, don't you? Huh Stacey? Tell me!" He kept asking until she answered him.

"Huh...aaahhhh.....yes." She whimpered. By now she was lost. Stacey thought she was pretty good in the sex department, even before she met Hank and during her marriage...but this, well, she thought, I've never had a cock like this. 'What am I saying????' 'But it feels soooooo dammnnnnn good' she answered herself.

"Want me to stop...huh...want me to pull this cock out?" He was taunting Her again.

She was lost to the amount of climaxes she had had by now...and she couldn't hold back the rest of them if she tried.

"Uh, aahhh. No, don't stop...don't.!"

"Then tell me...what do you want me to do to your cunt? Tell me."

"Fuck me...keep fucking me....please....fuck me good!" Stacey couldn't believe what she just said. 'Oh Hank...please forgive me....this is for you,' she said again to herself. Then she snapped back to what was happening.

The Black cop abruptly stopped, and pulled out of Stacey. When he did, she swore her cunt wasn't closing right away. She started to stand up, when he pushed her back down with her hands on the coffee table.

"I said keep your hands on the table Missy." He said, forcefully.

She did, and as she stayed there, bent over, he approached her from the front with his swollen cock in hand.

"Suck it Stacey, suck the best cock you've ever had! Keep your hubby outta jail." Stacey, not really having a choice in the matter, opened up her mouth and shut her eyes again. While he shoved his cock in her mouth, he damn near chocked her with it. Grabbing her hair on both sides of her head, he began to mouth fuck her...forcing it to hit the back of her throat with each thrust.

Stacey's curiosity got the best of her, and every once in a while, opened her eyes to see this black shaft fucking her mouth. With what seemed minutes, was actually seconds, and Stacey felt the head swell, and the shaft stiffen....and just then his cum shooting in her mouth.

"Aaaahhhhhh yeah baby! Oh yes......ah! Ah!" He hollered.

He again held his cock in one hand. This time, while still holding onto a clump of hair, pulled his cock out, and began to rub that Big Black Cock against her lips, cheeks and face as his cum was still oozing out of the tip.

"Yes baby....oh...you were really good. I knew you'd like it, once you got going. There's the bathroom, now get cleaned up so you can be well rested for the Judge tomorrow. I'll put in a good word for you, and who knows...maybe the Judge will have to "Judge" for himself."

***

Stacey, with shaky legs, slowly moved to the bathroom. Not wasting any time, she just plunged into the shower. Spitting the cum out of her mouth, she never felt like such a slut. Not that she didn't suck cock before...just that it was her husbands. As the water ran over her body, she started to relive the event that just unfolded. It was while lathering with soap across her neck, on top of her shoulders, her arms... and then her breast, she remembered what a wave of 'shocks' he put to her. While lathering her breast, she remembered how he tweaked her tits and caressed them so well....and the way he sucked on them. 'What am I crazy...are you going nuts Stacey' she said to herself. As she continued to wash, her hands guided themselves to the part that felt totally filled.....her pussy. As she looked down, it was slightly swollen, and a little pink. Probably from the size of that cock. 'I can't believe I took that thing...but it felt sooo good' she said to herself. And the way he talked to me...I mean, he knew...he just knew I'd want more of it, and like it as well. What is it with Him? There's something about his commanding of the situation. She came out of the bathroom, and the cop was gone. She checked the doors and window...sure enough...they were locked tight. She strolled into the bedroom and laid on the bed. She rolled her head to the nightstand, it was 11:18 pm.

***

Morning came, and Stacey woke up to silence in the house. At first she thought it was just a dream, but quickly realized it wasn't when she heard keys in the door, and it opening.

"Hey...time to wake up!" The Black cop hollered.

71

"Better get dressed, the Judge will be here in an hour!"

Stacey put her clothes on and sat on the couch...just waiting. What will happen to her...and her husband? Will that cop really tell the Judge? Will he put in a good word for her? Or was it all a lie?!

***

Shortly within the hour, give or take, Stacey heard the door being unlocked and then opened.

"The Judge here wants to talk to you first. I told him what you said about the drugs not being yours...but he wants to hear it for himself."

In walked this barrel of a man, about 6'4. He smiled and quietly said, "officer, leave us alone for a few moments… ok?" The door closed, and it was just the two of them.

"Now, tell me what happened" the Judge asked. Stacey, sometimes whimpering... and sometimes sobbing, and other times, out right crying, tried to piece the events together.

"Well, you know they have a solid case. Those packets alone will get your husband ten years. Because the car is HIS, and not yours, it would be hard to convict YOU...even though both of you were there." The Judge explained.

"But they weren't ours...honest" as she started to tremble and cry.

"Well listen, the Officer here tells me that you've been REAL cooperative. You really don't want your husband to go to prison...is that right?"

The Judge said, smiling, as he slid his hand over her nice firm ass.

'My God! Him too? I have to do it with him also?' She thought to herself.

"Meaning?" Stacey looked right at him.

"Well, let's just say that we can work this out. Then we can both be on our way. No record of it...understand?" the Judge said smiling bigger than ever. He took off and discarded his robe and threw it aside. With tears welling up again, Stacey knew she was without a choice.

The Judge began to discard his shirt, and wasted no time unbuckling his pants and throwing them to the side as well. Reaching out to Stacey, he cupped her breast.

"Yes, nice tits. I guess you get told that a lot… huh Stacey?" the Judge remarked. Now, Stacey, not wanting to be there much longer, began to undress as well. As the blouse dropped to the floor, and then the pants, she figured she might as well get it over with. The Judge wasn't in the best of shape, but at least not a slob. He had a hairy chest (which Stacey kinda liked in men), and as usual, a tent in his shorts. Before she could take off her bra and panties, the Judge put his hands on her shoulders, motioning her to her knees.

"The Officer here, tells me you suck some good cock. I'd like to get some of that." She was being forced down into position.

Stacey reached out and began to rub the bulge in his pants. It too felt large and thick. She reached in his boxers and felt something just about the size of her wrist.

'My God...do all the guys here have large cocks?' She thought to herself. When she pulled it out, sure enough, not only was it as big as the Black Cops dick, it was a tad bit thicker. She began to stroke it with her hand, building up her nerve...and then started to kiss the head. by now she had precum on it. Then she started to lick it, and eventually placed her lips over the end and began to give him his blow job.

"Oh yeah baby! That's it! Suck that cock! Damn, you are good!" The Judge sighed.

Somehow, Stacey was getting into it. Somehow, she was overcoming the fact that she was getting what she wanted...for her sex. These men wanted her, and were treating her like a slut, and after last night, not being hurt, began to get over the fact that she would do it. 'This can't be. I mean...I've seen videos of this and now I'm' she', flashed through her mind. After a few minutes of good cock sucking...the Judge laid on the floor, on his back.

"I'd get on top woman, but I don't want to crush you. Know what I Mean?" His shaft was as stiff as a board.

"Now that you've got it hard babe...how about straddling this cock and giving it all you've got. I'll Judge how well you do." Stacey slowly straddled his wide hips, and began to rub her cunt on his huge cock. Like the night before, she might not have been into this, but her body was disobeying her by having her cunt wet and ready. She knew this by the time she lowered herself onto his shaft.

"Uh, oh aahhh....yes! That's it! Put that pussy on this cock!" the Judge breathed heavy. "Damn girl...you're tight. Doesn't your 'ole man give you enough cock? That's alright, I'll change that. Go baby...ride my shaft. That's it...fuck it!"

By now Stacey was beside herself. Not only did she get over the soreness from the night before, she was enjoying being filled up again. She felt the head sliding up and down the walls of her pussy, and reaching deep, deep within her. Her pussy was ever so stretched by now, that taking this cock was nothing. By now, instead of her straddling him on her knees, she had risen herself up to her feet, and freely swinging her ass up and down....like a piston. She was shoving it in with much more pleasure like a total slut.

"Oh yeah baby....that's it...take that cock....you like it...you like that big cock...don't you. Fuck me...fuck yourself...go for it!" The Judge kept encouraging her. This went on for at least 25 minutes, with him and her changing positions. When he was on his knees, fucking her doggie style, Stacey was hollering, whimpering and at times begging for more.

"Yes...fuck me...oh God...fuck me with that cock....yes....jam it in me...put it in me.....fuck this pussy." She said over and over again. Somehow, she had forgotten why she was doing this in the first place. With a slap on her ass the Judge was taunting her now. "fuck this cock. That's it! Fuck it like the slut you really are!" With the Judge pounding her ass, slapping his balls against her cunt he shouted. "Officer...Officer...come here!"

With that, the door swung open, and the Black Cop appeared.

"Ms Stacey here said she'd like for us to forget about the whole incident. What do you think?" The Judge asked.

"I think I can help you make that decision Judge, but a few things will have to be cleared up first." The Officer said, stripping off his clothes. He knelt on the floor in front of her, and every time Stacey tried to reach up with her hand and grab his cock, he'd put it back down on the floor. "That's a good girl. Search it with your mouth....put your lips on it. Suck this black cock. You know you want it. huh Stacey?" "Yes!" She was panting. "Yes....give me that cock. I want it...give it to me...please!" She was so eager to say. With not one, but two big cocks in each end, the sparks and waves and waves of orgasms were overwhelming, and by now, Stacey couldn't control herself.

When it was time for the Judge to shoot his load, his spanking became more apparent, leaving her ass bright red.

"Yes...here it comes....aaaahhhhhhhhhhh… feel me fill you up, you little Slut!" He belittled her, as he indeed fill her up. The cum was dripping out of her pussy, down her leg after he pulled out.

"Switch!" The Black officer shouted.

With that, the two men switched positions. Standing her up, Stacey, was now bending over at the waist. The Judge by now just stood there with his hands on his hips, as Stacey took her left hand and started to not only stroke the fat cock, but was eager to suck on it as well. She was slurping, licking up and down the shaft, and at the base, would lick his balls as well. When the Black Cop entered her, she rolled her head around and just looked. After getting the fat cock from the Judge, anything would fit by now. She was enjoying the fucking she was getting from both men.

When she rolled her head back around to continue giving the Judge his blowjob, she noticed herself in a mirror on the bookcase. 'What a funny place to put a mirror' she thought. The view was something, yet erotic at the same time. Here she was...this lily white body, sandwiched between these two huge black bodies. She was fucking and sucking like some wild animal.

***

She was told to get dressed.

"Let her go, and get her 'ole man too. See...things DO have a way of working their way out...don't they?" The Judge remarked, smiling.

As she was getting ready to go, the Officer approached her with a handkerchief.

***

Cars were whizzing by, and every once in a while, there would be a bright flash.

Hank woke up, feeling groggy, like he had a hangover. He grabbed Stacey's arm, and lightly shook her.

"Honey… honey...wake up...wake up"

"Huh...what....who....Hank?" she said...startled.
I fell asleep, how about you? she said.

"Asleep...what about the cops?" Hank asked.

"What cops...Hank...you must be dreaming or something. This is where you said we were pulling over to catch a short nap. Your funny, honey" is all Stacey said.

"You drive, I'm getting in the back seat, and finish my sleep....are you going to be ok the rest of the way?" she asked.

"Yes honey....I'll be ok. If it's a dream....I guess that what it was then" Hank said back sheepishly.

Stacey crawled into the back seat, and pretended she was falling fast asleep. Under the cover of darkness, she slid her hand down her shorts as to double check. There, as she slid her fingers under her panties, the wetness was still there. Inserting two fingers in her pussy was easy, and when retrieving them… she put them in her mouth. There was no doubt that it wasn't a dream.

***

It was just getting dark, and Myra Ellerbee was on her way home. She was just a tad over the posted speed limit, when the two cops stopped her.

"Can I see some identification Ms" said the Black Officer.

Myra handed him the registration and her license. He walked to his car, and within two minutes, comes back.

Everything seems ok...mind if we take a look inside your trunk as well miss?" Remarked the officer.

"No… not at all." She said smiling.

He looks around, and drops two packets out of his sleeve into the floor of the trunk while she's not looking.

"Well, well, well.....what do we have here?"

Boss Man

I pulled into work and it was hot as hell outside. It was one of those stagnant days with no wind blowing and a layer of sweat you can't get rid of. I pulled into my usual parking spot around the corner from the parlor, grabbed my purse and headed for the front door. I had been working at this local ice cream parlor for about 6 months. It was one of those strip mall kind of shops that was open from 11 AM to 10 PM. I was the usual closer and was in charge of cleaning up after all the patrons. Mike was another kid that worked there with me; he was only there for two months. Together we closed the shop down 4 nights a week. I liked the job because it gave me extra spending money and allowed me to have some fun on the weekends.

I almost forgot to tell you a little about myself and what really happened two days ago. My name is Marcia and I am a 19-year-old freshman at a small private college 10 miles from the beach in South Carolina. The money I saved the summer after high school graduation was gone by October and I needed a job. I had a boyfriend in high school but after graduation we kind have went our separate ways. He was the one who I lost my virginity to and it wasn't that great of an experience to be blunt. I guess you could call it a quickly in my parents basement. I had been on the pill since I was 16 just because of the cramps, oh god the cramps. Well I have matured a lot since then, or at least I thought I had. I'm a college woman now, 19 and ready to take on the world. I'm a little tall 5'6, slender with really nice hips and weigh about 118 pounds. For the longest time I endured names like string bean. I am pretty skinny with B-cup breasts and a tomboy attitude, shoulder length dirty blond hair. I take pride in my neatly shaved pussy, with all that hot weather you have to do something. With a school at the beach you would think you would have a good tan. I rarely see the beach. Good thing there is a fake n' bake next door. I usually slip in once a week.

Listen to what happened a few days ago. Mike and I showed up at 4 o'clock and started our shift. The night was slow, just a few customers here and there. About quarter to ten the Owner showed up. I had not met him before but I knew his name was Tyrone Butler. Our supervisor told us he was hard to work for and had a shady reputation around town. He just stopped in the mornings to grab the money and head for the bank. Well I got nervous as this tall black man walked through the front door right before closing. Mr. Butler scared the shit out of me. He stands about 6 foot 4 and is built like one of those wrestlers. As my dad would say, he is as black as the ace of spades. Well he came in and went right to Mike and asked to see him in his office. About a minute later mike walked right out the door and didn't even look at me. From around the corner followed Mr. Butler and watched as the kid walked out. Then he looked at me and said now lock the front door and see me in my office. I was really nervous as I flipped the dead bolt over and walked into the back of the parlor. His office was small, just big enough for a desk and two chairs and a camera. I had never seen the camera and neither did mike. Mr. Butler told me to sit down and watch. There was mike on the screen taking money from the register. Just then Mr. Butler looked me strait in the eye and asked me how much I was making off with. I could not believe this as I snapped back and said, "there is no way I would steal money from you." He just looked at me and then he relaxed and sat down in the chair across from me. Our knees were almost touching as he shuffled some papers. HE smiled and said, "OK you're good and never late." I was relieved at that point and then the phone rang. It was our supervisor calling to tell Mr. Butler that he had to go out of town for a few days for a funeral. I just watched Mr. Butler as he talked on the phone. He was big and black. I glanced over him for a few seconds and noticed a limp monster under his mesh shorts. My pulse started to race and my hands got sweaty. I just thought of how big that thing could be. Stop it I told myself. Mr. Butler was pissed and said, "I will see you in five days", and then slammed down the phone. MR Butler looked at me and said, "well it looks like you are working with the boss for a few days". He said, "I'll see you tomorrow at 4." I got up, grabbed my purse and went out the back door, opened my car door and flopped down in the driver's seat. I just thought in my mind that I was going to have to work with this man for the next few days.

The next day I finished my classes around 3 and went home. Wednesdays are so long for me, class and then a long night at work. I stepped into the shower and melted away for 20 minutes. For work that day I was wearing an old parlor tee shirt, board shorts and a pair of vans. I put my hair up in a ponytail and left for work. On the way to work I thought about Mr. Butler and how I had to be on my best behavior. It was ten till and I walked through the front door and punched in. I walked in the back and there was Mr. Butler going over the books. I tossed my purse on his desk and told him I would be up front helping customers. I was out in the front for about a half hour when Mark came in the parlor. Mark was this guy I had a crush on but he had a girlfriend so it really didn't matter. I flirted with him for a few minutes when Mr. Butler poked his head around the corner and told me to mop the floor. Mark walked out and I picked up the mop. Mr. Butler helped the few customers that came in the store. I mopped the floor and soon finished the customer area and was now starting on the back area. I pushed the mop and bucket to the back of the shop and turned around to go back out to the service area. As I turned I slipped on the wet floor and crashed into the steel prep table. I started to cry due to the pain in my knee, it was unbearable. Mr. Butler heard me and came back picking me up off the floor. He sat me on the prep table and I clutched my knee. At this point the skin wasn't broken but it was throbbing like crazy.

Mr. Butler went back to his office and came back with a glass of water and a pill. He told me to take this pain killer. I think he called it a perkaset or something like that. He explained that when he was in college playing football he would get hurt and always kept a stash around. I took the pill and swallowed it down. He reached into the freezer and grabbed some ice. It was at that point he took off his parlor shirt revealing very muscular arms. I giggled and asked him if he always wore a wife beater. Mr. Butler was a sports trainer before he bought this chain of parlor stores. He wanted to take a look at my knee but some customers came in and he had to go out front. He was out there for a half hour or so when he finally came back to me. The Ice had made my knee numb and the painkiller was really working. I felt a bit tipsy but that was sure better than that throbbing pain.

Mr. Butler pulled up a stool and asked if he could have a look. I laid back resting my head on a towel as I stared up toward the ceiling with my legs dangling over the edge. He pulled the ice pack off my knee and slowly put his hands on my knee. He gently rubbed my knee back and forth checking it like a professional. As I stared up at the ceiling I couldn't help but think of him wearing those shorts the other day and what was in them. My mind was reeling and that pill had really kicked in. Mr. Butler was rubbing my knee and gradually his hands moved up a few inches to my lower thigh. I felt that feeling in my stomach tighten as I started to get really wet. Little did I know but Mr. Butler had a great view up my loose board shorts. With each rub of my thigh his grip stayed firm and felt great. My pussy was glistening and Mr. Butler just sat there working his way up my smooth thighs. I should stop this I thought, it's not right, a 40-year-old black man taking advantage of me but it felt so good. There he was sitting between my legs rubbing a thigh with each hand. His fingertips worked their way under the bottom of my shorts. His huge hands were just inches from my soaked pussy. I started breathing deeper, my god this was happening. He moved his hands all the way up under my shorts with his palms on the top of my upper thighs. He slowly moved his thumbs under the sides of my lace panties. As he touched his thumbs together over my pussy he noticed I was shaved bare. His grasp became firmer as he opened my pussy with his two thumbs. He slowly placed his thumb atop my clit and began to encircle it with slow circular motions. He slid his thumb into my pussy up to the knuckle. I took one deep breath and clenched my soaked lips down on his thumb. At this point I was in bliss. My nipples were poking strait up in the air and this man was working my pussy like I had never experienced before. Just then the bell rang and in walked two customers. Mr. Butler stood up and grabbed an apron, tying it around his waist to hide his growing erection. I heard him interact with the customers and after five or ten minutes they all left. I heard Mr. Butler walk up to the front door and turn the dead bolt and flip around the closed sign.

He was walking back and I lifted my head. As he came around the corner our eyes met. He walked up to the edge of the prep table between my legs. I was looking into his eyes and let out a little smile as

I lowered my head back down on the table. I guess this was the indication to him that he could do anything to me he wanted.

Mr. Butler peeled off his wife beater and sat down on the footstool once again. He reached up and grabbed the waistline of my shorts pulling them and my soaked panties off in one quick motion. He grabbed my hips pulling me up to the edge of the steel counter. I placed my bare feet on his broad shoulders and then slowly spread my thighs. I lifted my head up just in time to see him cover my entire pussy with his mouth. It was electric. I began to tingle all over as he swirled his tongue all over my clit and inside my pussy. I was groaning at this time as my hands were rubbing my firm stomach and fully aroused breasts.

Then he sat back and stood up with a massive erection poking through his mesh shorts. I leaned up on my elbows in a daze as he stood there. Then he dropped his shorts and out came the biggest blackest cock I had ever seen. He was twice the size of the boy who took my virginity. That monster was about 10 inches long. His precum glistened in the light. I reached out and wrapped my long white fingers around his massive cock. I sat up and with my other hand, cupped his balls. They were the size of pool balls; each one could sit in the palm of my hand.

Just then he pushed the stool up against the steel table and flipped me over on to my stomach. I could touch the stool just enough to lift my ass up in the air a few inches or so. I had forgotten all about my knee buy this time and was just accepting the fact that, my boss, a forty-year-old black man, was about to fuck the living shit out of me. He leaned up against me and I felt his pubic hair tickling my ass. His 10-inch cock was lying on the top of my ass crack and ended at the small of my back. I looked back at him and asked if he had any protection and he just laughed. I turned my head back around giving him the encouragement to proceed.

I felt both of his hands on my ass and then between my thighs. He opened my swollen pussy lips with his thumbs and leaned down and kissed the small of my back. I felt his cock head touch the entrance to my shaved pussy and took a deep breath. Mr. Butler grabbed the head of his cock and slowly moved it up and down, smearing his precum all over my swollen pussy lips. I was so wet he easily got five inches into me with one slow push. He pulled out slowly and then went back in a few more inches. My head was spinning. He wrapped his hands around my slim waist and was fucking me really deep. He was going slowly and it was driving me crazy but he still had three more inches to go. I looked down between my legs as this huge black man's cock was sliding in and out of my young pussy. I had never felt anything like this before. His huge balls were tickling my shaved pussy each time he entered me.

All of a sudden my head snapped back and he inserted his thumb in my ass up to his knuckle. My breasts were laying against that cold steel as I clutched the other side of the table. I was raising my ass up on my tiptoes to meet his thrust each and every time. He had grabbed my pony tail and pushed the small of my back down to the table. There I was face down on a steel table with this black bastard holding me by my pony tail with one hand while his other hand held me down across the crack of my ass. With one long thrust he lunged the entire length of his cock into the deep recesses of my pussy. He stayed still for a few seconds as my stretched white pussy tried to hold on for dear life. His mouth was an inch away from my ear as he whispered into my ear, "now I am going to fuck the shit out of your cute, little, white hot pussy!" He started to pick up the pace and was slamming into me. My pussy lips glistened as they were stretched around his big black cock. My cunt began to really tingle and I let out a whimper and then some increasing moans. A few hard strokes later I was grunting like a crazed slut. I was being literally fucked silly. I was about to have an orgasm as my pussy clenched down on his cock. The head of his penis was poking at my cervix and that drove me over the edge. I was Cuming. Mr. Butler leaned back down to my ear and whispered, "now I am going to fill your pussy with a ton of my black cum, I hope you're on that pill girl cause if you're not your going to be pregnant for sure." This started a second wave of orgasms and I looked him strait in the eyes and grunted, "Fuck yooooou." Then his huge balls tightened up and he pushed all the cock in that he could. His cock head was braced against my cervix when the first stream was injected into me. He pumped stream after stream of cum into my little pussy. As his orgasm slowed down he just stood there with his cock braced against my cervix. He just admired the sight of my little pussy lips wrapped around his cock, glistening in the light as they twitched with his cum matted all over my glossy pink pussy lips. I looked down at his balls that were trembling as they rested up against my pale shaven snatch. We stayed together like that for about a minute. As he pulled his cock out a huge stream of cum erupted from my pussy and ran down my leg into my panties and onto the floor.

He walked out to the front of the store and flopped the sign back and unlocked the door. HE walked pass me, slumped over the steel table with globs of his potent seed flowing from the depths of my stretched out cunt. He gave me a kiss on the fore head before speaking to me. "You have customers waiting."

I heard five people come through the front door. I slowly pulled up my cum filled panties snug and tight, then my shorts. I slowly walked out to the front of the shop, barely able to put one foot in front of the other, to help those who were waiting. I felt like I was floating.

For the next two days his cum drained from my pussy. He fucked me three more times that day and stretched out my pussy so much that it just gaped open from there on. I had become a black cock craving whore almost overnight.

Curing The headache

I get home from work and find Kathy watching Wimbledon on my TV. She has decided to stay for an extra week or two. I haven't decided whether it's because of what happened a couple of weeks ago or because she loves tennis and I have digital TV and she can therefore choose which match she wants to watch.

I get in, put my coat away and walk through to the living room. "Hi, Kathy. Good day?"

"No, not really. Got a bad headache. Just felt like sitting here watching the tennis."

"Okay, fine. Can I get you anything, or can you hang on until dinner."

"Dinner'll be fine, but I may not eat much."

"No problem."

I go off for a shower and afterward come back just as Kathy is changing matches and going back to Centre Court. The black American female tennis player, Chanda Rubin is playing, and it's then it strikes me just how much she looks like Kathy. In fact, if I couldn't see Kathy sitting right in front of me on the settee, then I would be sure she had quickly travelled up to Wimbledon, got into some tennis gear and was now posing as the American player.

"Feeling any better?"

"No, but I know something that will help a lot, but I'll need your help."

"Of course, whatever I can do."

"Okay. Just sit here and I'll be back in a minute. But you have to promise me one thing."

"Sure."

"No matter what I do in the next half an hour, you are not to move, complain, stop or otherwise impede me. Okay?"

Slightly hesitantly I agree and Kathy walks off to the closet where my coats and shoes are kept. "Right," she says as she walks back through, "Just keep watching the television screen."

"Well, that's not a problem as you seem to be playing on Centre Court. Where did you find that dress, it really accentuates your fig..." All of a sudden it goes dark, and I realise that Kathy has put something over my eyes. She has really thought it out because whatever it is has completely blocked my vision, even the two small holes you usually get because of the material not fitting round the bridge of the nose are covered. Once I get over the surprise of the loss of sight I realise that I can't hear Kathy moving about, the only thing I can hear is that Chanda Rubin has just won a point.

A minute or so later Kathy voice comes from just in front of me. "Right, remember what I said. You are not to move, complain or stop me doing this okay? In fact sit on your hands!" she commands.

"Erm, okay." I stand up slightly and place my hands on the settee cushion and then sit down again. It's quite effective for stopping you from using them as your own weight seems to trap them into the settee.

"Okay, now just sit back and relax."

I settle back into the chair, wondering what is going to happen next. It's at times like these you really do realise just how much you use your eyes and how without them you are so disoriented.

I feel Kathy's hands on the waistband of my trousers as she finds and undoes the clasp. I then feel the trousers loosening as she undoes the zipper. I'm intrigued but decide not to say anything.

Next, one of Kathy's hands slides into the slit in my boxers, finding my flaccid penis, she takes hold and releases it from my shorts so that it feels as though it is sticking up through the slit. This has the instant effect of making my blood rush to my cock and I can feel it starting to stiffen slightly. I feel one of Kathy's fingers gently stroking my cock. It runs up the slowly hardening shaft to the top and then down the other side and round my balls.

As my manhood grows and stiffens I can feel Kathy using two fingers, then three, all gently stroking me and making me grow harder and bigger with each stroke. Then, gently she cups my ball sack and I feel something soft and moist on the tip of my cock. From past experience I can assume it's her tongue. Using her lips and teeth she delicately pushes my foreskin down and exposes the sensitive tip, her tongue gently licking and sending waves of pleasure through my whole body. I give a little sigh.

"Enjoying it?"

"Mmm, yes."

"Well, let's see what you think of the next stage."

I wait, eyes blinded, with anticipation, excitement and nervousness all rolled into one. Then suddenly I feel a strange substance that seems to be wrapping itself around my dick. It doesn't feel like liquid, but it's not a solid either. It feels as though it is slowly moving down my shaft and I am not sure if I like the feel of it. My cock reacts in agreement and starts to lose its hardness. The substance still runs down my deflating cock and I can feel it slowly running down onto my balls now. It is so hard to describe the sensation or guess at what it could be.

Kathy must guess why my body is reacting in the way it is, because she says "Don't like it? Oh dear that's a shame. It's my own headache mixture. I've always found it works. It's a special mixture of honey and crushed aspirin."

Well, that explains the strange feel of it, why it doesn't feel like a liquid or a solid. It's amazing just how much you lose when your sight is gone.

"And what I intend to is give myself this special headache mixture by licking it all off until you are clean."

That does it! My cock regains it stiffness in double quick time. The thought of Kathy licking me, with or without honey, is enough to send it into overdrive.

"Ha ha! You like the thought of that, then?" She must see how I've reacted to the thought. "I guessed you might. Would you like to try some of my special mixture?"

I nod my head.

"Open wide."

I open my mouth and Kathy inserts her finger allowing it to come to rest on my tongue. I can taste the sweet honey and it's wonderful. To think she is about to lick this off me only increases my hardening cock.

"Would you like a little more?" She asks as she removes her finger after allowing me to lick it clean.

I nod again.

"Okay. Open wide and lean forward a bit."

I do as she asks and then feel her soft, cool silky skin as it brushes my face.

"Take a lick."

I reach out with my tongue and find the unmistakable shape of her nipple covered with the honey. God, she must be at least topless. That thought alone sends shivers right down to the tip of my cock. I gently start to lick and all the time I feel my manhood growing harder and larger. I never thought I could get as much pleasure from Kathy without actually seeing her, but this is something else.

"Make sure it's all gone."

I continue to lick around her erecting nipple and place gentle kisses around the base ensuring that any honey left is licked up. I sit there enjoying the sensation of kissing and licking her breast without being able to see it. My cock reacts in agreement.

As soon as I can find no more honey to lick, although I wouldn't mind, I enjoy the taste of Kathy's tits, she removes it from my mouth and gives me a gentle push so that I am sitting back in the settee.

"Now, you know what I am going to be doing, and what it tastes like."

I wait for a second, two seconds, three seconds and then, ahhh, that it's so good. Kathy's tongue touches the base of my cock and slowly rises up the shaft to the tip, I can only assume she is licking off the honey as she goes as it still feels wet from her moist tongue.

Another lick, slow and purposeful, gently raising from base to tip and making me grow harder.

Another, this time starting a little further down on my ball sack. Slowly up to the base of my cock and then up and up and up. This time is different. At the tip she stops and then suddenly I feel my cock engulfed within her mouth. I feel her lips running down the sides and her teeth gently stroking as my cock gets harder and she pushes further down, getting my shaft deep into her mouth.

Then up. Slowly she reverses the direction and her mouth rides up and her lips take the honey with them leaving my penis with a thin coating of her saliva.

Now down. Oh God, this feels so good. I so want to see her sucking my cock that it is all I can do from not whipping off whatever it is she has placed over my eyes.

Up. Slightly faster now, and her hand cups my balls and slowly starts to massage and gently squeeze them. God, this feels so fantastic.

Kathy give's a little moan and I guess she must be enjoying this as much as me.

She stops. I wonder what is going to happen next? For a few seconds nothing seems to happen and the sound of the television drifts back to me. I had completely forgot it was on. A minute or so later, Kathy says "Okay, take your blindfold off."

I raise my body off my hands and take off the blindfold to be greeted by the sight of Kathy laying completely naked and her chocolate brown skin covered from the base of her neck to the top of her bush by a meandering trail of honey. Oh Christ, this sight is so erotic that I can only just stop myself grabbing my cock and releasing the tension that has been building up since she started this "special headache cure".

"Would you like some more honey? Well, get out of those clothes and come and get it."

Quickly, I remove my shirt, trousers, socks and gingerly take off my boxers, trying not to get any last residue of the honey from my cock on to them. I then sit down next to where Kathy is laying.

"God, that honey looks better on you than me. I guess it must just disappear on my white skin."

"Shut up and enjoy." She answers, laying completely flat and leaving her body completely open to me.

I continue to look, just taking in her beautiful brown body with honey dripping down from her neck, between and over her full breasts, covering both nipples, sliding down the underside of her right tit, over her flat stomach and just stopping short of her bush. I am torn between diving right in and just sitting and admiring the sight before me.

I decide what to do and gently lower my mouth to Kathy's and we kiss gently. I kiss her again but this time slightly below and to the side of her mouth. I start to make a chain of kisses running from her mouth down to the top of her neck, each kiss slightly below the last, Kathy giving little moans of encouragement, until I find the start of the honey trail. I place a small kiss on the start of the trail, but let my tongue come out and gently lick up the honey. I move down a few centimetres and repeat the action, all the time getting closer to her dark brown cleavage and all the time my cock reacting to the sight, smell and taste of Kathy mixed with the honey. She encourages me on with increasing sighs and moans.

I reach the top of her left breast, the trail inviting me to work my way down to her dark brown nipple sitting erect on her tit. I continue to work down the brown fleshy globe gently following the line of honey. And then, there it is, her nipple sitting proud and erect, covered with the sweet sticky substance. I can't resist, just the sight of it makes me harden and grow. My tongue comes out to lick the small cone free of the honey and then I place my lips over it and gently massage and nip it with my tongue and teeth. Kathy's moans increase and she adds a few gasps to the mix. I glance up at her as my lips, teeth and tongue play and see her head back and eyes closed.

I notice Kathy's hand slowly stroking her stomach, each stroke getting closer to her centre. I watch her hand, mesmerised as it moves closer and closer. She raises her legs so her feet are flat on the floor and the tips of her fingers disappear between her thighs, and still she continues to stroke herself. I slowly move my mouth from her nipple, continuing to following the sticky trail across the underside of her breast and on meeting her arm, which is laid between her full tits, place a gentle kiss on her elbow before continuing over to her right side and upon finding the honey trail again slowly travel to her right nipple, it also sitting erect surrounded by the wonderful liquid.

I close my lips around the chocolate brown button of flesh and start to tease it as well as lick the honey surrounding it. Kathy's hand continues to explore between her legs, her groans continuing to increase. My cock grows in unison with her volume. I love hearing her getting pleasure.

Then a gasp and I realise she has entered herself. The tips of her fingers will be slowly disappearing within her and finding her clit.

Another gasp and a sigh as she obviously finds it and starts to play and tease herself.

I split my concentration between watching her wrist, which is all I can see from this level, and sucking her nipple clean.

Kathy's breathing increases, her groans become gasps and shouts. From within her I can hear her heart beat increase and her body starts to shiver as waves of pleasure start to build from her centre. Her wrist moves quicker with each stroke, she has to be going deeper and still massaging her clit. My manhood really starts to throb and I want to empty my load on to her.

This thought makes my legs and arms weak. I cannot keep kneeling over her like this, I am going to fall on top of her. I lift my mouth from her breast, placing one last kiss as I lean back and watch her body convulse with the sheer pleasure of her wanking. Her eyes closed and although in a frown I can see a look of ecstasy in her face. Her hand quickens still, my cock and balls grow heavy with the weight of the seamen stored within me. "Oh Christ," I yell, "Let me come as well!" I raise my hand to my cock, but Kathy's free hand flashes out and on finding my leg works her way up it. I guide her hand up to my cock and her long, dark fingers wrap themselves around my shaft and she starts to wank me as well as herself.

Her hand on my cock moves in motion with her hand at her cunt. She quickens both hands and from her shouts and screams (thank God there is no one living next door at the moment), I can tell she is not far from climaxing. From the throbbing in my cock and balls and the weakness in my legs I know that I am not far from it either.

Still Kathy makes both her hands go faster and suddenly her back arches, her body raises in the air and she lets out a loud scream. At the very same moment she gives my shaft a final fast stroke and my hot seamen shoots out of the end and down on to her body. My body shivers as the fluid flows out and down across Kathy, the milky white fluid glistening on her brown skin.

Kathy's body stays arched as she is determined to get every last second of pleasure from both her climax and my cum on her body.

I look down and see her as her body relaxes. My juice on her neck, breasts, across her arm and down over her stomach, slowly mingling with the honey.

Kathy's back returns to the floor and slowly she opens her eyes and looks up at me. "How do you like my headache cure?" She asks "And it really works, you know. My headache has completely gone."

Deep South Slut
Part 1

Major and Mrs. Stephen Wilson had been married 9 months. The Major had enlisted in the North Carolina 3rd Militia shortly after the start of the civil War, in May of 1861. He'd been away from his new bride Emily for almost 8 months. He has written several times a week and his most recent letter was delivered in the previous day's post.

Emily Wilson continued to live on her family's large cotton plantation. As her darling Stephen prepared for war, it was decided that she should return to her parents to await the quick end of the war. She had grown up here and known no other home. This classic plantation home had wide porches on both levels that wrapped around the entire home. As with most southern homes, the home had several servants who cared for the needs of the family, providing the cooking, cleaning and other services as needed.

Emily awoke early in the morning, still distressed by the contents of Stephen's most recent letter. The graphic sexual nature seemed so unlike the southern gentleman that she grew up with and came to love. His words, so vile, had shocked her, but in a strange way had excited her to the point of a restless night. Stephen had never used words like cock, pussy, and cunt. Ladies and gentlemen didn't speak that way. She was shocked by his vivid descriptions of sexual practices. Apparently the topic of discussion at the officer's mess turned to sexual relations and the experiences of the others were significantly more worldly than the Wilson's had ever dreamed of.

Emily's sleepless night had mostly focused on a passage of Stephen's letter that described a practice of sucking the semen from a cock and using a tongue to stimulate a clit. Emily and Stephen's courtship had lasted 3 years. They had enjoyed gently playing with each other's privates. Could she say that she had enjoyed the feel of his cock? She loved to play with it, to feel the veins that ran along it, to feel it harden at her gentle touch. She loved the way he would play with her breasts, squeezing them, gently sucking the hard nipples; his soft fingers teasing her. She still remembers the day he first touched her privates. His hands, roamed her body wildly, touching her everywhere. He seemed fascinated by her soft brown hair, the moistness between her legs at her slippery wet cunt. He rubbed her as she did the same. They ended that and most other evenings quickly departing before either reached their orgasm. They were fearful of crossing a line that ladies and gentlemen never crossed.

She had later learned that by removing most of her pubic hair, Stephen was less distracted and paid more attention to her clitoris and vagina. She had sharpened her father's straight razor and gently removed her hair. Stephen was shocked, but the constant attention to her pulsing clit had resulted in her first orgasm for each of them together.

Shortly after that the war started and they decided to marry before he enlisted. The wedding had been wonderful, the joining of two great southern family's. Her wedding night was the first time she got to feel his strong cock enter her waiting pussy. Fortunately she had been an avid horseback rider and her hymen had long ago been broken. Oh the fun they had during that month. She had grown to love the fullness of his cock. He had made love to her on the veranda one evening under a full moon. The two had become excellent lovers.

She was confused by the way her body betrayed her. She wanted to be upset about his language in Stephen's letter, but she found herself using the same words as she reminisced about their sexual relationship. Had she lived in a too sheltered life? Were some of the things Stephen wrote about really acceptable loving acts shared by a husband and wife? Would Stephen really lick her cunt, tease her clit with that tongue she loved to kiss? Could she touch his cock with her mouth, kiss it, lick it, suck it and most of all take his sperm from it into her mouth? All questions she wasn't sure about. He talked about many other acts that interested her, but by far these had her greatest attention.

She continued to lay in bed, dressed in a sheer nightgown, gently playing with her protruding nipples. She longed for his touch. She needed to feel him inside her, thrusting and sweating with her in their soft, marriage bed. She gently let her fingers dance across her abdomen to reach the soft tuft of brown hair in her groin. She had given up trying to trim it when Stephen shipped out. She hadn't even teased her clit until a month ago, when lust overtook her after reading one of Stephen's passionate letters. Her fingers now had reached her clit now and all she could think about was Stephen's cock sliding in and out of her. Pounding her deeply, grinding his pelvic bone against her throbbing clit. She let out a moan as her heart beat quickly and uncontrollably.

She continued to lay on top of her bed sheets, rubbing her aching pussy dreaming of the gentle way Stephen might tease her with his tongue as her heart slowed. She was shocked to open her eyes to see her slave Oscar standing in the room, with his hat in front of him staring at her sweating body with one of her hands gently playing with her exposed cunt. He apologized for disturbing her, but he was planning to ask her if she still wanted to go for her morning horseback ride, when he heard her moan and came right in. She quickly covered herself with her sheer nightgown, realizing that it didn't hide her; she then reached for the sheet. She told Oscar that she would be out in a few minutes and to saddle her horse for a ride. He withdrew from her room, as he turned to walk away, she could see the large tent in the front of his trousers. How long had he watched her playing with herself?

She quickly dressed and headed to the stables for her ride. Riding had always been a release for Emily. She couldn't be bothered to ride sidesaddle; she preferred to ride like her father. She could jump fences and gallop across fields with her strong legs wrapped around her trusty horse bullet. She had her first orgasm five years ago, riding bullet. The grinding of her pelvic bone against the leather saddle, the changing gate of the horse beneath her all could produce an amazing orgasm most days. As her clit was already enflamed, she thought today would be one of those days.

She rode for miles and miles through the fields, never seeing another soul. Throughout her ride, she continued to think of Stephen and her love life. She thought of the day she had been playing with Stephen before they were married. As she jacked him off a drop of his cum had landed on her best dress. Without thinking, she had carefully lifted the drop with her manicured fingernail and put her finger in her mouth. She remembered the taste, salty, but not vile. She loved the musty way Stephen smelled when he returned from the fields, the taste of his sweat. She loved the way his cock felt in her hand, soft yet hard. She knew she wanted to lick him, but was very worried about taking his cock in her mouth. Would she choke, or worse gag?

As she rode, she fantasized about many things. Taking that cock in her mouth and loving it. Having her clit licked and teased. Her imagination was running wild as her body enjoyed orgasm after orgasm riding bullet across the fields. Her thoughts turned to Oscar and his erection in her room this morning. She wondered if he had jacked off thinking of her. Did he dream of pleasing her? Did he have a big cock? Could she practice sucking cock using Oscar? Would he lick her pulsing pussy and make her cum? That pushed her over the edge she had to stop riding and walk the horse for a while. Her panties were soaked; the saddle even had a wet spot.

She loved the thought that she had turned on Oscar. It was very taboo for her to even think about him in that way, but she had heard the stories of the sexual escapades throughout the South between white men and women and their slaves. She wasn't in love with Oscar; she just wanted his cock and tongue to play with. As he wasn't really a man, she rationalized; it wouldn't even be cheating on Stephen. She would just be practicing some skills to please him with after the war. She knew she was turned on by Oscar; he was tall and very muscular. A light skinned black man, well groomed, always clean. Judging by the tent she saw in his trousers today very well endowed. She set out a plan to lure him in to play with her.

Emily plotted the entire way home. As she arrived at the stables, Oscar took immediate care of the horse as she dismounted. He would wash the horse and feed him as was part of his responsibilities. She knew the wet spot on the saddle was bigger than before. She drew Oscar's attention to it and asked if he could clean her saddle later today. She turned and walked to the big house, pausing once she turned the corner. As she suspected, Oscar nose was in the seat of her saddle inhaling the musky odor she had left behind. The tenting in his trousers was quickly back, oh how she wanted to suck that cock. She reentered the barn; it was Oscars turn to be in a compromising position. She found him with his right hand in the front of his pants stroking his cock. Without commenting on it, she asked if he could draw her some hot water for a bath as she was all sweaty from her ride. He said he would get right on it as he slowly removed his hand from his throbbing cock.

Emily returned to her room and removed her riding clothing. She had on a thin robe that didn't reach her knees. It was loosely tied in front, her large breasts were clearly visible from the sides. The house was empty with the exception of Oscar. Her parents had taken the cook and the maid servant into town for most of the day. Emily lightly teased her clit as she stood near the tub and waited for Oscar to return with the water warming on the stove. He added the first batch of hot water to the cold water in the tub. She had sent Oscar back to warm more water, and left the door open for the cool summer breeze. She slipped the robe off her shoulders and ran her hands down her body as she stepped into the tub. She was a fine looking woman, lean with large breasts and shapely hips. The water in the tub didn't even cover her pubic hair, yet she lounged back and awaited Oscar to 'find' her in the tub. As expected, 15 minutes later, he walked to the tub with another large bucket of hot water. As he walked down the hall he was shocked to see her sitting in the tub. She was usually very modest and he was only able to catch a passing glimpse of her beautiful body. Today she sat naked in front of him. Her nipples were brown and clearly excited. He could see the patch of brown hair above the water line. She waved for him to come in in order to pour the water. His pants were struggling to contain his erection.

With her delicate fingers, she reached up and untied the length of rope that had served as his belt for many years as he poured the water. He was shocked and just stood there not saying a word. She slowly undid the buttons. His cock sprang out as it wasn't contained by any underwear. It was magnificent, about the same size as her Stephen, but black as coal and perhaps a bit thicker. As his pants fell to the floor, Oscar stood motionless; convinced his wildest fantasy was coming true. Emily ran her hand along the length of Oscar's cock, paying special attention to the joining of the head to the shaft. This had always excited Stephen. Her plan was working better than expected. She continued to hold tightly to his cock, raised herself up on her knees in the tub and turned to face his cock. In her other hand she held a warm washcloth and slowly washed the length of his cock and his balls and to prepare him to be devoured.

After rinsing him off Emily spoke to Oscar. She said she needed his help in a very personal way. Based on his reaction, he would enjoy himself. She told him he would need to let her practice anything she wanted to do on him. He would be told, by her, exactly what he was to do and he should do nothing he wasn't told to do or she would have him beaten. He readily accepted because at that moment, her tongue was tracing a line down the shaft of his member toward the tip. She grasped the shaft with her right hand and opened her mouth to accept the head of his prick. She moved her tongue around the head as if she were French kissing it. Oscar moaned as she accepted more and more of his cock and her hand slid faster and faster along the shaft. Emily realized that she controlled his every action. Her fear of choking was gone, but what would happen when he came?

The silence was broken as Oscar said, "Ms. Emily, if you be keeping that up, I be shooting in yo mouth, maam". She broke her lock on the head of his cock long enough to say that was exactly where he was to shoot his load. That was all the encouragement he needed as she resumed her tongue assault on his cock. He started to tremble and she felt a twitch from his balls as the first spurt landed in her mouth. It was quickly followed by a second, but she had to pull him out and the third landed on her cheek. A fourth steam of cum landed on her left breast as she continued to jack him off. His cum was salty and thick. It was different than she expected, but not unpleasant. Some of his load had begun to leak from the corner of her mouth and she reached for the wash cloth to wipe it away as well as her cheek and tit. She continued to hold most of his load in her mouth, playing with it with her tongue, tasting it and moving it around before she finally deposited it in the wash cloth.

She gave Oscar's cock one final stroke and told him she was done with him for now. He should dress and return to the barn and wait for her. Her parents were due home any time and she wouldn't want to be caught by them in a compromising position.

With one of her questions answered, she relaxed in the tub and began to dream about Oscar tonguing her pussy and teasing her clit. Emily drifted off to sleep in the tub until awoken by her mother Elizabeth's movement in the house. Emily was wrapped in a towel when her mother entered her room. Elizabeth's eyes were immediately drawn to a trail of dried cum on her daughter's neck. Obviously Emily had learned some of the many pleasures that the slaves could provide; she thought to herself as she headed back out of the room. Elizabeth decided she would share some stories of her own escapades with Emily in the days ahead.

Part 2

As Emily dressed, she could not stop thinking of the experience of sucking Oscar's cock while she was in the tub. She loved the way it felt, so hard, yet so soft. She loved feeling it respond to every move with her tongue. She loved the feeling of being in control of Oscar, the power she had over him was better than she could have imagined. She controlled his climax, delayed it, and when she was ready, caused it to erupt. She loved the feeling of his cum in her mouth, so thick and salty.

She was shocked at the sheer pleasure she derived from this sexual act. She couldn't wait to slip away and demand additional services with Oscar the slave. She hadn't given his race, or the taboo nature of the pleasure a second thought, all she could think about was having that tongue attack her delicate clit. She wished her plan at enticing Oscar could have already resulted in some direct excitement for her, but that would come, and judging by the excitement she was once again feeling it would come soon.

As Emily finished tying the bow on her dress, she began to reread her husband's most recent letter with great interest. She skipped over the pleasantries from her soldier husband and focused on the erotic acts that he related in his letter. She had already decided that Oscar would be made to service her clit with his tongue, that wasn't an issue; rather, she was focusing on the wide ranging other procedures that were discussed. She fantasized about trying each and every one with Oscar, vowing to have her beloved Steven return from the war to a much more worldly and experienced lover able to satisfy his every desire.

In the meantime, Oscar had returned to the barn. He was still trying to absorb the blow job he experienced from the lovely Ms. Emily. She had been a vivid fantasy of his from his adolescence. He had been purchased by her father when he was just a boy. He was spared the life of a field hand and assigned to serve as a stable boy and inside servant when necessary. She was just a few years younger than him. With her love of riding, had been a frequent guest to the stables where Oscar spent his days.

He was thinking back to all the fantasies he had over the years of Ms. Emily sucking his cock, her lily white face making a perfect contrast to his hard, black manhood. He had spent many a night dreaming of shooting his load in her delicate mouth. Today's events were even better than his best fantasy. Just as he was beginning to stroke his cock, his girl Ruby entered the stable. She loved the site of him playing with himself and found herself on her knees wrapping her lips around his rock hard dick without saying a word.

She was devouring him, and he was fucking her face harder than he had ever fucked it. He wrapped his hands around her head and pulled himself deeper into her mouth. The harder he pushed, the harder she sucked, licked and jacked his cock, until he finally shot his load deep in her mouth. She gently licked him until he was clean, licking her own lips at the pleasure of having his cock in her mouth, before she spoke to him. She asked him what he was thinking jerking himself off in the stables in the middle of the day. She sat down next to him on a bale of hay, as he told her the story of Ms. Emily's blowjob.

Ruby had been owned by Major Steven's family, given to the newlyweds as one of the wedding gifts from the groom's parents. She was a beautiful woman with chocolate brown skin, a beautiful face and a body that few could compete with. She was perfectly shaped, every man's fantasy woman and many men, both white and black had experienced the joy of her body.

The Major's own father had been a frequent visitor in her shack. He liked to bend her over the bed and fuck her hard from behind. The Major had also been a frequent guest in her shack. Ruby had taught him all he knew about sex, her body was his plaything. He had fucked her every way imaginable, and a few ways that defied gravity and imagination. All those frustrating sessions with the prim and proper Ms. Emily, ended with Mr. Steven fucking Ruby until he was satisfied. Ms. Emily may have been saving herself for marriage, but the Major liked a good hard fuck, and wouldn't have tolerated Ms. Emily's cock teasing if he hadn't had Ruby to fuck after he took her home. Ruby wasn't surprised when she was given to the newlyweds after Mr. Steven's father had walked into her shack one night while his son was receiving a blow job from Ruby.

Since moving to Emily's parent's plantation, Ruby and Oscar had become the main source of the family's entertainment. Both Ms. Elizabeth, Emily's mom and her father, Mr. Robert had discovered the beauty of Ruby and Oscar. When they were together, they could please each other all night. Gently moving from one position to another; never speaking, just moving in perfect unison. As much as Robert and Elizabeth enjoyed the show, it was the participation that they found most exciting. Ms. Elizabeth enjoyed the power of Oscar's tongue, particularly while watching her husband fucking Ruby. Both couples would often spend the entire evening in the shack, watching, fucking and sucking until all were exhausted.

Ruby laughed thinking that Ms. Emily was finally growing up and beginning to explore her own sexuality. Ruby would love to teach her a few things. She could teach her how to please a man. She could teach her how to please a woman too. Just how much had Ms. Emily desired to learn? Ruby heard Ms. Emily talking to her horse bullet in the outside stable and decided to give Oscar one last kiss and climb into the hay loft for a 'bird's eye' view of what might transpire.

Ruby had just settled into a comfortable position when Ms. Emily walked into the barn. She walked directly to Oscar and reminded him that she needed his assistance and she expected him to obey her every demand. Oscar, of course, agreed that he would do anything she asked, she just needed to say what she wanted and Oscar would see she enjoyed it. All she could manage to say was that she was in need of a good licking. Oscar immediately understood and walked over to a shelf on the wall and retrieved a red horse blanket for Ms. Emily to sit on.

Oscar spread the blanket on a hay bale and directed Ms. Emily to sit on the edge. Her fancy blue hoop skirt was a sharp contrast against the rough wool blanket and the hay and straw in the barn. He found himself on his knees, looking under the big hoop skirt and the layers of petticoats and other garments he would have to make his way through to satisfy her desire. His rough hands found the inside of her calves and slowly caressed his way up to her thighs when he was confronted by yet another undergarment.

Emily was on fire from his first touch to her ankle. He was so strong and muscular, even his calloused hands were sending shock waves up her entire body with each new inch of her skin he explored. When he reached her undergarments, she raised her hips from the hay bale and Oscar quickly pushed them to her ankles. He was almost completely covered by her hoop skirt, with only his lower legs and feet visible over her skirt. She could feel his hot breath on her thighs as he caressed the back of her knees and traced a line along her inner thigh. She could feel the moisture building in her pussy. She had waited for this licking all morning, and now she was ready to see if it would feel as good as she imagined it.

He began his oral attack slowly, using his tongue to trace lines on her upper thigh; he could smell her scent combined with the aroma of lye soap. He continued to restrain himself from attacking her clit and probing the depths of her pussy. He would have plenty of time for that. For now, he would focus on teasing her and taking it slowly so as not to scare her off.

Emily was growing tired of the delicate approach and asked Oscar if he knew exactly where she wanted to be licked. Without waiting for an answer, the delicate Ms. Emily grabbed Oscar's head under her skirt and pushed it directly over her throbbing pussy. Not one to misunderstand a subtle hint, Oscar began to lick and suck her pussy with a fury that caused Emily to gasp. He was licking the entire length of her, from her ass to her clit, and oh how he played with her clit. She was on fire; her juices were flowing as she approached her orgasm. Being a delicate southern belle, Emily was normally very in control when she came, but this was quite a different kind of climax. She was pushing Oscar's head into her clit as his tongue was repeatedly flicking and teasing that little friend. She was moaning and telling Oscar to suck her harder, when she first felt his rough fingers enter her delicate pussy. He was pounding in and out of her with his skilled hands while never taking his tongue from her clit. She was juicy, and he loved the feeling control he had over her, hearing her moan, feeling her pussy quiver, all made him want to send her over the edge.

It only took a few more strokes, and Ms. Emily had the orgasm she so desired. It was a loud and sweaty one. She was thrusting her hips to meet Oscars tongue as he finally pushed her over the edge, her entire body was shaking and her pussy was pulsating as she was lost in the moment. She tried to catch her breath, but the sensations went on and on as Oscar had not stopped his gentle treatment of her throbbing clit. Oh how she needed that!

Ruby must have been in need as well, because from Oscar's first entry under the skirt of Ms. Emily, Ruby's long and slender fingers had been teasing her own clit. She had often experienced the pleasure of Oscar's tongue and she knew the joy that Ms. Emily was feeling. She remembered back to the first time she had been eaten by Oscar. She had been so wet that her juices soaked his shirt as she came hard on that wonderful tongue of his. As Ruby continued to lightly play with herself, she could see Oscar remove himself from under Ms. Emily's petticoats. His cock looked so hard, trying to be restrained in those old worn out pants. She half expected to see him pop a few buttons with the strength of that powerful dick. Emily straightened herself, pulling her undergarments back into place. She thanked Oscar for his service, asked him not to tell anyone about their interlude and told him she had some other items she would need his help with in the next few days. He told Ms. Emily that she only needed to ask, and he would see that her needs were met.

As Emily turned to leave the barn, Ruby knew that her own needs wouldn't be able to wait. As soon as she thought Ms. Emily was out of hearing shot, she called to Oscar to get that blanket and his ass up to her, she needed a good hard fucking after watching the little princess be eaten out. Oscar grabbed the blanket and headed for the ladder to the hay loft. Upon reaching the top of the ladder, he was met by the warm embrace of Ruby. They kissed deeply, Emily's juices covering both their faces. Ruby told Oscar she needed some of the same attention as Ms. Emily had received, but she wanted his hard cock in her afterward. She sure needed some serious cunt plowing.

Once again, the red horse blanket was spread out, and this time Ruby laid down on it, raising her knees and pulling back her own simple skirt revealing her exposed pussy. Her lips were already puffy from her finger's attention, as Oscar dove right in and began to play with her enflamed clit. She loved that skilled tongue and in what seemed like no time at all he had pushed her over the edge to another wonderful orgasm. Now all she could think about was that hard cock driving deep into her eager snatch.

She pulled his head from her pussy and brought him to her. Kissing him deeply, she told him she needed a good hard fuck. Oscar took one hand and unbuttoned his trousers, pushing them down just far enough to free his aching cock. No additional foreplay was needed, both lovers knew what they desired was not slow, or gentle, but rather hard and fast, a pounding they would both enjoy. Oscar's cock was brought to Ruby's waiting cunt and with one fluid motion; he was buried all the way in her. She gasped at the fullness, she would never get used to the size and skill with which he could use his tool. Oscar began to thrust like a jungle beast. Ruby grabbed his ass and pulled him in to her. She wrapped her long slender legs around his waist and pulled him even deeper. He was moving in and out of her with great skill as the lovers exchanged another passionate kiss. All the fluids mixed together in their mouths. All they could taste or smell was pure raw sex.

His pounding continued as he could feel Ruby's orgasm build. She was breathing harder and harder, her legs were pulling him deeper and deeper, and her pussy muscles had clamped down so tightly around his cock that with each thrust, he wondered if he would be able to pull his dick out for another thrust. With one final thrust, both lovers came, sending stream after stream of his cum deep into her pulsing pussy. Ruby and Oscar's bodies were dripping in sweat from their intense copulation. Their embrace tightened and they held each other until their breathing slowed.

The lovers shared one final kiss. Hot and steamy would be an understatement. Their embrace relaxed and their tongues danced as the lovers were once again wrapped up in the heat of the moment. They finally parted, knowing that their pleasure would likely be repeated this evening and wondering the extent to which Ms. Emily's personal exploration would please the couple in the days ahead.

Part 3

As Emily gathered herself together in the barn, she was amazed at how alive her body felt. The pounding in her chest, her heavy breathing were sending her to a new awareness of her bodily urges. She loved how Oscar had known how to bring pleasure to her body. She was glad she opened her legs and allowed herself to feel his teasing tongue. She had worried she could not cross the line with Oscar and let him between her soft thighs. But Emily never hesitated, and Oscar had been so skilled with his tongue. She had no regrets, she wanted it all.

Emily wondered if he had the same level of skill with that wonderful, large dick of his. She had so enjoyed holding it in her hand, feeling it stiffen under her gentle touch. She thought back to the wash tub and stroking the full length of his eight inches with her delicate fingers, barely able to close her hand around its girth. Would she ever allow herself to indulge her pussy with that powerful black tool? She longed to have him plow into her, reaching those places in her pussy left untouched since the departure of her beloved Stephen.

Emily had so many questions. Her body had never had such desire. Could she let Oscar fuck her pussy? Would she open her legs and let him place that hard black cock at the opening of her cunt and beg him to drive it into her. Could she give herself to another man? Her rationalization that Oscar was somehow less than a man was strained now that she had let him suck the juices from her pussy. He had licked her delicate clit until she was too far gone. If he had taken his tongue from her clit and placed his cock at the opening to her cunt; she knew she would have wrapped her legs around him and pulled him in. She would have enjoyed every inch of him, felt the sweat on his muscular chest and stroked his strong black body with her lily white hands. She knew she was ready to fulfill her desires. No regrets, just pure animal pleasure.

Arriving back at the house, Emily found her mother packing a bag. Elizabeth's sister Juliet had taken ill and sent word to Robert and Elizabeth that she needed their immediate assistance in managing her plantation. Elizabeth had considered inviting Emily to join them, but thought her place was on their homestead, continuing her sexual experimentation. So, Emily's parents announced their departure for a week. If they left immediately, they could reach Juliet's plantation before sunset. Bags were quickly packed and Emily said goodbye to her father. Elizabeth wanted to speak with Emily privately before they left.

Elizabeth carefully chose her words as she sat on the sofa in the parlor with Emily. She wanted to find a way to encourage her daughter's exploration. She decided to place her education in the hands of Ruby, the upstairs maid. As she gently touched her daughter's shoulder, she simply said that she understood that she was experiencing new feelings and they were a healthy development of a young woman her age. She should enjoy every new experience and if she needed guidance or found herself with questions she should turn to Ruby.

Elizabeth went on to say that Ruby was experienced in the ways of the world, a warm and compassionate woman and most suited to help her in any way possible. She told her daughter that she had confided in Ruby and she had always kept her confidence. Emily was shocked by her mother's words, had her pleasure with Oscar been so transparent that she knew what she has been doing today? She hugged her mother goodbye, telling her that she would talk to Ruby if she found the need. Emily watched from the front porch as her parents buggy traveled down the drive with a cloud of dust stirred in its wake.

Emily sat on the porch and thought of what the next week might hold for her. Would she turn to Ruby as her mother had suggested? Could she talk about such matters with a slave girl? Ruby was not much older than herself; could she really be so skilled in the ways of the world? What lessons could she learn from another woman? The only lesson she wanted of was Oscar fucking her needy pussy. Oh, what she wanted him to do to her with that black tool of his. Just thinking of it brought a smile to her face. Emily sat on the porch and daydreamed for the rest of the afternoon, slowly sipping a mint julep trying to quench the heat of the afternoon sun.

Sarah the cook had prepared the evening meal for Emily, it was delicious. As the meal ended with dessert, Emily's tongue was never so sensitive; the strawberries so juicy, the melon so sweet. The juices ran from the corner of her lips reminding her of the warm semen Oscar had deposited in her mouth that morning. She had never enjoyed fruit salad to this level. She longed for her beloved Stephen. Would he coat her body in the wonderful assortment of fruits and juices devour her body, inch by glorious inch? Her body would be at the mercy of his wonderful tongue.

Emily could feel her moisture building. Her clit was on fire, longing for the touch of Stephen. Oh, what he could do to her body. She would submit completely to his every wish. He could penetrate her however and whenever he wished, she would gladly accept him in her mouth, pussy, or even her ass, if that would give him pleasure. She needed that wonderful cock of his.

She found herself comparing the dimensions of her husband's member and that of Oscar the slave. Except for the dramatic difference in the color, they were both very similar. Same length and girth; both men seemed to be skilled in the use of the tools. What they could do together to her body caused a shiver down her spine. Would Stephen ever allow Oscar to share their bed? Could both men service her body at the same time? To have a cock in her mouth and one in her pussy, she would be in heaven. Could she get them to cum at the same time? To get them to climax in her mouth and her cunt at the same time would be divine.

After dinner, Emily re-read her letter from Stephen. All of those acts that initially sounded so vile now caused her to feel even more excited. She wanted to try them all. She wanted to feel the pleasure of each and every act that he listed. She had never had a day so full of fantasy and excitement. She was in desperate need of a good, hard screwing. She knew since mid-day that would be the only thing to satisfy her desire. She began to draft a new letter to Stephen, but she struggled to put into words her feelings since receiving his letter. Amazed how that one letter had changed her outlook and began her self-exploration.

Would he be proud of her or disappointed in her weakness and angered by her turning to a slave for sexual satisfaction? She wondered if Stephen had ever sought out a slave for his personal enjoyment. Had he ever let a slave girl suck his cock and sent his load into her pretty mouth? Ruby was beautiful, had Stephen ever seen her naked and ever fucked her?

Ruby was so shapely, Emily found herself dreaming of what a beauty she must be without her clothes. Emily had never seen another woman naked. She was wondering how soft her breasts must be, how wet her pussy must get when it was gently stroked. How tight was her cunt when it was penetrated and filled. Emily was amazed that she was once again getting wet. This time, she was dreaming about Ruby's beauty. She was very confused by her desires. Would she find pleasure in Ruby's touch? Would Ruby find pleasure in Emily's touch? Could another woman's tongue ever make her clit dance the way Oscar's had? Would another woman's cunt feel as soft and giving as her own? Could she have an orgasm by the tongue of another woman? These were questions that disturbed Emily.

When the sun had set, Emily left the house and headed to the slave compound. She needed to be fucked by Oscar. She had to feel that cock buried deep in her. She did not need any more foreplay; this had been a day of foreplay. She didn't need to be made love to; she needed to be mounted and drilled until her body had the satisfaction it had been screaming for all day.

Upon reaching Oscar's shack, she could see the lamp burning in the window. Emily was very self-conscious of her choice to come here tonight. She worried what the slaves would say about her being here if her true intentions were known. She thought she would peek inside to make sure he was alone before knocking and demanding him to penetrate her.

She was shocked at what she saw. A beautiful naked slave girl was lying on her back on a straw mat on the floor, with Oscar's muscular body on top of her. He was licking at her pussy, while she was sucking on his beautiful cock. Actually a better description would be he was fucking her mouth. Sliding the entire length of his cock in and out of her mouth, she seemed to be letting the length of him slide down her throat. It was hard to see the face of the girl, but she was clearly making Oscar very happy. She had his testicles in one hand and was teasing his asshole with her other. The more he moved, the more she played with him. Likewise, he was devouring her pussy. She had her legs spread, and he was using both hands and his mouth to eat her. She could tell by the quickening pace of his thrusts into her mouth that he was about to cum. She must have been also close as her legs had closed around his head, and she was thrusting up to meet his tongue's every move.

Upon seeing this display, Emily had put her left hand between the buttons on her dress, and was playing with her right nipple, squeezing it with every observed thrust. Her right hand had opened several buttons lower on her dress, and slid under her undergarments into her moistness. Her hands were stroking herself as she watched the lovers through the window. Oh, how she wished he was fucking her throat and licking her pussy. She was overwhelmed by desire. She never felt so in need.

Emily played with her clit until she was just about to cum; holding off her own climax for Oscar's penetration later, the whole time watching Oscar pounding that beauty and waiting for him to cum down her throat. Finally, his pace quickened, she could hear the moaning coming from inside as they came together. Each breathed deeply and teased until the powerful orgasms subsided, as Oscar shifted his weight, and removed his softening cock, beautiful Ruby came into clear sight.

Emily continued to stroke her clit, as she watched Ruby's naked form sit up and look toward the window and smile. Emily continued to tease herself, soaking in the beauty of Ruby, until Ruby licked her lips and raised her hand to wave Emily in. Emily's heart skipped a beat as she realized they could see her playing with herself, watching them. She slowly pulled her hand from her breast; she then withdrew her other hand from her clit after one final stroke, her fingers glistening in the candle light. She shivered with the idea that they had seen her play with herself. She thought of how radically her simple world had changed, as she drew her moistened fingers into her mouth and seductively licked them.

Leaving her dress buttons open, she stepped to the doorway, and with her dry hand turned the knob and walked inside without any idea of what to say to them. All of her inhibitions had left her; every nerve ending in her body was tingling as she slowly walked without a clue as to what would happen. As she entered the shack, Emily was overcome by the heat in the room on this stifling night. The aroma of sweat and sex permeated the entire room. As she entered, Ruby and Oscar made no attempt to hide their sweaty naked bodies, Oscar walked toward Emily with his arms outstretched. Emily's body failed her and she fainted from the heat and prolonged excitement she had endured.

Emily awoke with a start. She could tell by a soft candle burning in the corner, she was in her own bed. She could feel a hard cock nestled along the slit of her pussy, as she lay on her left side. Her right hand was holding the abdomen of a naked woman, her body sandwiched between Oscar and Ruby. All were naked. How long had she been here? What had they done to her body? Did she enjoy it? Could they do it again while she was conscious?

Emily slowly used her right hand to softly caress the sleeping Ruby. She could feel the swell of her Ruby's breasts. They were bigger than hers, soft and pliable to the touch. Emily could feel her hardening nipples and the gentle movement of her chest rising and falling with each breath. Emily's hand trembled as she explored lower on her abdomen. Finding a soft patch of pubic hair not unlike hers, she moved her attention to Ruby's upper thighs. So soft, she could feel her pussy become even wetter as she explored the beautiful shape of Ruby. Oscar wasn't talking, just slowly sliding along the outside edge of her pussy lips. His cock was soaked in her moisture. It felt so good to have a hard cock tease her clit with every stroke.

Ruby was wide awake, enjoying the small circles Emily's fingers were tracing on her upper thigh. She felt the warmth of Emily's flesh all along her back. And as each circle drew closer and closer to her pussy, it became harder and harder to lay still and enjoy. At the same time Emily found her own pussy attempting to capture Oscar's cock on each gentle thrust. She could stand no more teasing, she had endured countless orgasms today dreaming of Oscar shoving his cock into her and giving her the fucking she needed.

She couldn't take another passing of that beautiful cock at the entrance to her cunt and not buried inside. In one movement, Emily rolled onto her back, pushing Oscar and his lovely cock from her soft ass. She proceeded to announce that she needed a good fucking and that if Oscar wasn't man enough to handle the task, she would go find some other horny slave to ram it too her. Oscar needed no more encouragement, as he found himself between her shapely legs, his cock protruding in front of him as he approached her pussy lips with his juice covered cock.

She needed no more teasing, no more torture. He found her moist pussy and buried himself all the way in. She moaned loudly at the size and depth of his thrust. She begged him to fuck her hard and fast. She needed all of his cock sliding in and out of her. Over and over Oscar plunged into the depths of Emily's body; with each thrust another moan escaped. Ruby had rolled over; missing Emily's teasing and found the pretty white girl's nipples too irresistible to pass up. She played with her left tit and then sucked it into her hungry mouth. Emily had reached up and taken her other nipple in her right hand and squeezed the nipple harder than she thought she could endure. Her other hand found Ruby's soft back and gently caressed it as she began to moan from the powerful sensations in her clit as Oscar's pelvic bone crushed her own stimulating her clit with each penetration.

Thrust after wonderful thrust, Emily neared the orgasm she had waited for. She had never spent an entire day fantasizing about getting fucked like this. The sensations were all too strong, and she began to feel her pussy pulsate with each and every thrust. As Oscar pounded the delicate girl's pussy, she teased her own tit and played with Ruby's back. She was in heaven when she finally was pushed over the top and experienced a wonderful, heart stopping orgasm, feeling jolt after jolt of Oscar's cum as it splashed deep in her womb. She squeezed every muscle she could squeeze to hold Oscar's hard cock deep in her. She wanted this cum to last forever. It was an act of utter lust and she'd enjoyed every second of it.

Part 4

Miss Emily finally released her hold on Oscar's member, and it slipped from her warm moist cunt, leaving a trail of white cum on her upper thigh. She felt the weight of Oscar's muscular body shift on the bed, and then stand nearby. Before Emily could say a word, she could feel Ruby's soft hands continuing to roam her body, leaving her breast, her fingertips dancing across her belly and onto her upper thigh. She could feel Oscar's cum being smoothed into her skin by the delicate fingers of the beautiful slave girl lying next to her. Her finger's danced through Emily's pubic hair, oh so close to her inflamed clit. Just when she thought Ruby's fingers would brush against it, she felt a cool wet cloth begin to cleanse her sweat covered body at her toes.

Ruby shifted in the bed and was now standing on the opposite side of the bed as both Oscar and Ruby each had a cool, water soaked cloth. Each was gently cleansing a foot, a soft gentle touch on her right, a firm manly touch on her left. Each was moving up and down a calf, each cooling her overheated skin on this hot and steamy night. As if on cue, both cloths were removed and dipped in the basin near the bed, only to return to her thighs. The cool water dripped from the cloths, and ran around her thighs further dampening the sweaty bed sheets. Emily couldn't say a word as the trail of cum was washed from her skin. The cool cloths were so calming, so refreshing, Emily couldn't imagine a better way to cool off on this stifling hot evening.

Once again, both cloths were dipped in the cool basin, this time one returned to her slit while the other forcefully cleaned her pubic hair which had become all matted by the evening's activities. The cloth felt like silk sliding up and down her pussy, the touch so light, it almost faded away at times. A long slender finger was inserted into her cunt to wash away the remnants of Oscar's load. The finger felt more slender than her own, even wrapped in the cool wet cloth. She felt so clean, so cool she couldn't do anything, but moan and shiver as a peaceful calm came over her entire body.

Oscar's cooling efforts had left Emily's pelvic region and was now clearly focused on her luscious breasts. His strong hands were circling the outer tissues of her breasts, avoiding her sensitive nipples. Ruby was continuing to cleanse Emily's slit, now focused on a small trail of cum that had coated the region near Emily's asshole. Emily brought her knees in and lifted her seat from the bed to make Ruby's efforts easier. Ruby dipped her cloth in the basin and returned her attention the Emily's rear end. She used her free hand to pull her cheeks apart and then ran the cool, wet cloth along the entire crease of her ass. Emily moaned at the sensation of her ass being teased by the fingertip of this beautiful woman. Ruby's caress lingered at her asshole, circling the opening, teasing Emily who was surprised by her body's response to stimulation there.

Oscar had once again dipped his cloth in the basin, this time focusing on Emily's underarm region. What a strangely sensual feeling Emily thought. Ruby gently pulled her attention from Emily's rear end and having rinsed her cloth focused on her other underarm. The cloths seemed to move in unison as they ventured down the length of her arm, to the palm of her hand. Finally each finger was caressed. Emily was completely cooled, and more relaxed than she had been since receiving Stephen's letter.

Emily felt her lace eyelet cover gently placed over her naked body, as she saw in the shadows the two black figures turn to leave the room. Emily was unsure what if anything she could say to the two slaves that had given her such a night of pleasure. She simply said thank you and rolled over, grabbed her down pillow and drifted off to sleep.

Oscar and Ruby walked naked from the main house back to Oscar's shack. This wasn't the first time they had made this walk naked. While Oscar was pleased that he had finally fucked his fantasy girl, Ruby remained horny, demanding that Oscar eat her pussy. Once back at the shack, she laid herself back on the mat, and Oscar took his familiar place between her legs. She was wetter than he could ever remember her. Her aroma was musky, a combination of her excitement and sweat from the walk back to the slave compound. Oscar's skilled tongue began to tease Ruby's upper thighs and outer lips. She put both hands on the back of his head and directed his tongue to her throbbing clit. Oscar's tongue worked it magic and within a few minutes of constant attention, Ruby was squirming on the floor, her hips thrusting her cunt further into Oscar's mouth. Oscar was sucking her juices as fast has he could, stroking and stroking that clit with his tongue until Ruby finally screamed out in ecstasy. Her pussy quivered with the orgasm.

Giving Oscar no time to rest, she demanded that he put his eight inch cock in her and fuck her hard. As the tip of Oscar's cock reached her moist, waiting lips, he could still feel the pulsations of her orgasm. He buried his cock in all the way and began to pound away at Ruby's needy cunt. As his piston pumped in an out of her, Oscar's pelvic bone continued to grind Ruby's clit with each penetration. She was thinking about her hand deep in Ms Emily's cunt as her body gave way with another screaming orgasm. Oscar could stand no more, and pumped stream after stream of his hot juice deep into Ruby's steamy pussy. The lovers embraced, rolling Oscar on to the bottom, with Ruby resting her tired head on his muscular chest and drifting off to sleep with his cock still deep within her.

Emily slept later that morning than she had since she was a teenager. She dreamed more vividly than she had in years. As she slowly woke, the sun was high in the sky, and the slaves of the plantation were all hard at work. Ruby, it appeared, had already cleaned most of her room without disturbing her sleep. Emily smiled when she looked at her partially covered naked body. Small specks of skin were visible through the eyelets of the cover. Even her breasts were uncovered. She laid her head back on her pillow and began to draft her letter to her beloved husband so far away in the war. She had so much to tell him, but she struggled for the right words to tease and excite him with a much more adventurous sex life they would enjoy once he his service to the Rebels is complete.

Emily rose from her bed, choosing to put a light robe over her shoulders, but not tying the belt. She had always been so modest, she enjoyed having her body on display, she couldn't wait for Ruby to come make the bed, and find her breasts and pussy so on display. Emily sat at the desk in her room, putting on paper some of her thoughts for her letter to Stephen. She wanted to carefully choose her words; to excite him without upsetting him and raising his ire. She longed for his touch. As satisfied as she was last night by the efforts of Oscar and Ruby, she wanted so badly for her body to enjoy the pleasure of Stephen's body. She wanted to show him all she had learned about pleasure. All she would learn in the days ahead with the continued help of Ruby and Oscar.

She finally finished her letter, it was shorter than she expected, but it made her point:

Dearest Stephen,

I read with great excitement your letter dated November 5th, such interesting mealtime conversation. I long for your touch and the chance to learn to be the ideal wife. I can't think of anything I would rather do than please you. You may feel free to enumerate any or all of those items you mentioned that would give you pleasure, so I may satisfy your needs on your return.

I have learned a great deal about my body and yearn for the day I can once again share it with you my love. Stay safe and know that I am counting the days until you are once again in my arms.

Your Loving Wife,

Emily

Emily read and re-read the letter. Not wanting to be too bold, but at the same time, wanting to tease and excite her soldier husband. She wanted to make his eight inch cock come alive at the prospect of her taking his cock in her mouth and sucking him off. To be hard at night dreaming of taking her to the river, swimming naked and fucking her in the outdoors shortly after their swim. Emily wanted Stephen to dream of bending her over and ramming his cock deep in her pussy from behind. Beautiful Ruby could join them in their marital bed; Stephen eating one woman as he fucks the other. To have her pussy eaten raw, while she sucks Oscar's cock. The possibilities are endless. Each sounds more exciting than the last. Emily can see herself performing each and every act Stephen wrote about, and best of all, experiencing orgasm after orgasm as she fulfills her husbands every fantasy.

Emily put her letter in an envelope, and went to the dining room for some breakfast. As Emily was dining, Ruby had returned to her room to finish making her bed. Ruby saw the letter on the desk and opened it to read the contents. Slaves of their day were not taught to read, but Ruby was able to exchange certain favors to young Stephen in exchange for his secretly teaching her to read and write. Ruby laughed to herself at the simple language. Still afraid to tell the man she wants to suck his cock. Still too uptight to tell him she will take him in the ass. Ruby picked up a pen and added a short note to the bottom of the letter. It simply read:

Stephen, this wife of yours will be trained by the best. Expect her to open her legs at your command and fulfill your every desire.
I need your hard cock too.
Ruby

With that addition, Ruby sealed the envelope and left it where it was. Hoping Emily wouldn't realize that she hadn't sealed it earlier. Ruby finished her work upstairs and returned to the slave compound for the noon meal and to share the news of the letter with Oscar. Emily finished her breakfast and returned to her room to change into her riding clothes. She carried the letter to town, never noticing that it had been sealed by Ruby.

Emily posted her letter to Stephen, and returned to the plantation on her trusty horse Bullet. As she rode, she dreamed of sucking Oscar's cock again. Maybe she would just drop to her knees in the stable and suck that cock that had given her such pleasure last night. Would Oscar be surprised by her boldness? Could she do it? Right there in the barn for everyone to see. She had let Oscar lick her pussy in the barn yesterday. The stride of the horse and reliving the images of yesterday's sexual adventures lead to the building of an orgasm for Emily during the ride home.

As she dismounted Bullet in the barn, he was quickly taken by Oscar. Oscar would wash and brush him before putting him in the stable for the rest of the day. Oscar began to walk bullet away when Emily called to Oscar to let that wait, she needed him for a few minutes. Oscar tied Bullet up, and returned to where Emily had dismounted. Emily fell to her knees and untied Oscar's belt and began to unbutton his trousers. She said she never got to thank him for doing her so well last night and she wanted to feel his cock in her mouth again. Oscar, a man with few words, said nothing as Ms. Emily stroked his cock with her delicate white fingers. Teasing the tip of his black cock with her outstretched tongue before sucking his cock into her waiting mouth, Emily used her right hand to stroke his cock in and out of her mouth. Her fingers were barely able to wrap around the girth of that wonderful cock. With each stroke, Emily took Oscar's cock deeper and deeper into her mouth. Stroking him faster and faster, longing for his cum.

As Oscar looked down at the beauty at his feet, he knew he wouldn't be able to stand much more of her oral assault on his cock. The moistness and warmth of her mouth reminded him of being buried in her cunt last night. Of the sweet taste of her pussy and how horny all last night's activities got Ruby.

Oscar gave Emily no warning as stream after stream of his cum blasted into her waiting mouth. To Oscar's shock, most of his cum went down her throat. What remained, she appeared to be keeping in her mouth as she wiped her lips and rose to a standing position. She reached up, wrapped her arms around the neck of the strong black man, and kissed him on the neck, leaving a trail of his own cum on his neck. When she was finished, she told him to have Ruby, lick that off for him and then tell Ruby come find her, she turned and walked back to the main house. Oscar left Bullet tied up and set of for the slave compound to find Ruby.

Ruby was pleased to lick up the residue left from Ms Emily's blowjob on Oscar's neck. She was encouraged by the white girl's new found boldness and couldn't wait to get a taste of her sweet nectar. She wanted to see that little one squeal at the delight of a woman's tongue.

Emily wasn't sure what she wanted, but she needed to talk to Ruby and discuss all that she needed to learn about pleasing a man. What could she learn from this woman? Why had her mother been so confident that she was a wealth of information? What did her mother know about Ruby? What experiences did her mother share with Ruby? Would Ruby touch her again? She had been so delicate with that cool cloth last night. Her fingers felt great as she teased her body. Would Emily find the strength to touch her? Could she cross that line? Could she ever open her legs for a woman to eat her? How much would she learn from that educated tongue?

Holiday Adventure
Part 1

There is a psychological malady prevalent in the northern tier of the Rocky Mountain States--Idaho, Montana, Wyoming, and the Dakotas. It generally surfaces around mid-February--if not sooner--and can last into early June. Its symptoms range from mild irritation over things which would otherwise go unnoticed, to bouts of severe depression, to actually going out of your fuckin' mind. In other parts of the country, I'm sure it is known by different names. In our part of the country, it is commonly called Cabin Fever.

Cabin Fever has two root causes. The main contributing factor is the weather. Inside a well-insulated home it may be warm and toasty, but the weather outside (per ye olde Christmas song) is frightful. The high mountain winds drive the falling snow sideways with such force that it feels like icy needles piercing any negligently exposed area of skin, while, at the same time, the computed wind chill factor is sending the temperature straight into the minus double digits.

The second root cause is directly influenced by the first. Unless there is an absolute need to be outdoors, any reasonably sensible person is forced to remain indoors as much as possible. I, personally, don't consider skiers to be in the category of sensible persons. Sliding down a snow-covered hill on a pair of slats, dodging trees and praying you don't sail off a cliff into the wild blue yonder is not my idea of reasonable intelligence. But, as I said, this is a personal opinion.

If you are among those who enjoy horseback riding, fishing, camping, swimming, or a myriad of other summer time activities, winter in the Rockies is an impatient time of year. If, on the other hand, you happen to be one of us who enjoys a leisurely walk over hill and dale on a warm, pleasant summer day chasing after an elusive white ball, being regulated to The Golf Channel from early October to late May boarders on being an abysmal state of affairs.

Such were the conditions in mid-February when my husband came home from work with a proposition he knew I wouldn't... No, make that which he knew I couldn't refuse.

***

However, before I regale you with anymore of my story--not to mention its impending naughtiness, how about if I toss in a little background? Just so you can begin to picture some of the players in my bawdy play...and a couple of the non-players, too.

My name is Elizabeth. Liz, in all but the most proper of occasions. I stand 5' 9" and weight approximately... Well, that's none of your damned business. But, just so you won't think I'm being evasive because I'm overweight, uncouth...and even some couth...men wolf-whistle when I walk by. I've even overheard more than few women expressing their admiration of my figure at parties, and later in the evening, I've even been propositioned by a few of those same ladies. You want to talk about

143

flattery? I've come to expected that sort of crass behavior from certain men, but to have a supposed "proper" lady brazenly tell you she would like nothing more than to take you upstairs and cunt-lap you into unconsciousness, now that's being flattered all to hell, gentlemen.

Anyway, I have shoulder length dark brunette hair, my eyes are brown and my nose is straight, so are my pearly whites. My measurements are 37-26-36 and I fill a C cup. My areolas are a dusty brown and roughly the size of Mexican pesos. My nipples...when they're perked up and ready for action...have been measured at three-quarters of an inch in length with a dark reddish hue. The outer lips of my pussy, when fully aroused, become swollen and are hot to the touch, and they hold the most wonderful blush you've ever seen. My unhooded, shimmering pink clit (when it's engorged with hot, demanding lust) is nearly the same turgid length as my plump, aching nipples.

I am also that rare woman in this day and age (or so it seems) who prefers the furry covering Mother Nature has provided me when I'm au-natural, so does my husband. Therefore, the thick bush of coal-black hair between my long legs is trimmed only enough (and only in the summer) so that I won't gross out prudish people when I wear a bikini. Try picturing the actress Angie Harmon, without the throaty voice, not quite so squared-off a jaw line, and generally showing off far more deep cleavage, and you'll have an approximate mental image of yours truly.

Now to my dear, sweet hubby, my Caveman/Poophead. His real name is Randy and he stands six-foot even and weighs in at a solid hundred and seventy-five pounds. He has slate-blue eyes and short-cropped blond hair. He also has slow, practiced hands and a perfectly shaped...meaning just the right amount of curvature...seven-inch cock. Make of those last two useful attributes what you will, ladies. I certainly do...and as often as I possibly can. When it comes to Randy's lovemaking skills, I guess you could call me an insatiable glutton.

When we're not otherwise occupied (doing everything and anything we can to satisfy one another's heated lusts), Randy is an architectural engineer and I'm a legal researcher for a well-respected firm. This is a job I do mostly with a computer. Since any good computer, and also a reliable DSL line, will do, I work out of our home, which works out well for both the company and me. I'm not taking up valuable office space, and I don't have to travel the treacherous roads in the winter.

Randy and I are both in our early thirties and have been married for ten years. We don't have kids. Not yet. The sex between us, while no longer in the experimental stage, is still the best I've ever known. And Randy says, so far, he hasn't got any complaints, either.

So, you should now have at least somewhat of a handle on two of the players in this drama. Now, where was I? Oh, yes...

***

It was a cold and snowy February night when hubby came home with an irresistible proposition: A week down in southern Nevada, out of the snow and cold, playing golf. "And my big, smart, considerate hubby came up with this golf-get-away all by his lil ol' self?" I coquettishly inquired in my very best Ol' Virginny drawl.

Horsing around with each other is one of the ways Randy and I keep from going for each other's throats when the golf courses are under three feet of snow. He can horseplay just as well as I can, he just can't pull up the various accents and local idioms the way I can. Of course, he didn't have the balls to get up in front of people and perform like I did when we were both attending USC.

"Not entirely," he confessed as he hung up his heavy sheepskin coat. "I ran into Greg at the dinner this afternoon and he happened to mention that this new client of his had gotten his wife new clubs for Christmas and that she's chomping at the bit to do more then putt her way around the living room."

I waited for him to finish struggling with his overshoes. "And?"

"And... Well, Barb got Greg that new driver, and I gave you that new putter, so putting two and two and two all together, Greg and I figured..." Frustrated, Randy glared up at me. "Damnit, Liz, do you like the idea, or not?"

I finished setting the table then I gave my ingeniously conniving hubby my most beguiling smile and responded in Americanized Yiddish. "And vat's not to like about it?"

Over dinner, Randy filled me in on what he knew about Greg's new client. Aside from his name, Derrick Thorne, and that his wife's name was Darcy, it amounted to next to nothing. Other than the fact that they obviously played fairly expensive golf. For those of who don't know, custom-fitted Ping golf clubs do not come cheap.

Derrick Thorne?" The name was vaguely familiar to me.

It was to me, too," Randy said with that irritatingly smug smile of his when he knows something I should. "He was a defensive back for Dallas. I thought he was pretty good, but they apparently didn't. He only lasted five years with the Cowboys and never got picked up by anyone else."

"There could be any number of reasons why he didn't sign with another team," I pointed out.

"Generally, it's because they're more trouble to a team off the field than they're worth to them out on it. They're either into under the counter substances or they're up on spousal abuse charges. Could be that their behavior in public is entirely too outrageous, or they've had too many DUIs. Stuff like that can reflect badly on the team as a whole and bottom-line owners are really cracking down on it these days."

I was aware of all of this, but something--call it a hunch, or woman's intuition--told me none of this behavior stuff was the reason Derrick Thorne wasn't playing pro ball anymore. As I was stacking the dishes next to the sink for Randy (When he cooks, I wash. Since I cooked this night, he had to wash.) I had an inspiration. "How about we scrounge up another couple to go along. That would give us two foursomes."

"Who you got in mind, Liz?"

I thought about that for a long moment. With January babies, both the Russell's and the Simpson's were automatically eliminated. "How about asking Vera and Ron?"

"They really don't play up to our game, Honey." Randy made a sour face. "Besides, I don't like Ron all that much. He's too ah..."

"He's too much of a spineless worm," I less politely finished for him. "But, I like Vera, and I really do enjoy playing with her. And so does Barb."

After giving this due consideration---all of about sixty seconds since we both knew we didn't have a ready-to-go forth choice...Randy relented. "All right. You call Vera while I finish with the dishes."

Hearing him mumble, "If I'm lucky, Ron won't be able to get the time off," I smiled to myself as I picked up the phone. Just the day before Vera had said how she wanted to get away for a few days, and that Ron had the time available for them to do it.

"God, yes!" Vera gushed when I told what we had in mind. "If I don't get out of this frozen wasteland, for just a couple of days, I'm going to tear my hair out, by its black roots."

"Don't you think you should check with Ron before committing to this?"

"Probably," she sighed. "Okay. I'll call you back and let you know what he said." Her voice became a lot more determined than it usually is. "But I'll tell you right now, we're going with you guys, or else."

Vera is one of those unlucky individuals who truly suffers the psychological tortures of Cabin Fever, so getting the hell out of here for even a few days would be a true godsend to her, before she actually did tear her hair out by its black roots. Loosing any of the dark hair on top of her head would not be a good for Vera; it's thin enough as is. Though, the dark pubic hair between her legs is a thick, overgrown thatch. We had showered together at the golf course often enough, so I've seen the tangled jungle below her outtie bellybutton. I had even commented on its unruliness one afternoon as we dressed at our lockers, that it could do with some judicious snipping and plucking here and there, or at least a little grooming now and then.

"Whatever for, Liz?" she had responded in a listless voice. "Except for you saying something about it just now, no one else seems all that interested in the sorry state of affairs between my skinny legs."

I had laughed, as much to mask my slight embarrassment at this awkward moment as to what she had said. It wasn't so much what she had said, but the way in which she had so nonchalantly delivered her last line. Vera can be very funny at times, in a dry sort of way.

***

Okay, I can see where this might be a good time for another background check. Ron and Vera are our over-the-backyard-fence neighbors. Vera stands five foot five inches and weighs all of a hundred and five pounds, maybe a hundred and ten when she bloated at that time of the month. With 34b boobs and hips that are almost boyish, saying her figure was petite would be putting it generously. I mean, she really doesn't need to wear a bra in public and has confessed to me that she rarely does so around the house. Over half the surface of her breast is dark areola and her nipples--even in a relaxed state are unusually elongated.

Vera, like me, is a natural brunette, though hers is even a couple shades darker than mine is. She wears her thin--bordering on just this side of being stringy--hair in a short pageboy. She has thick eyebrows over dark eyes, has a pug nose, slightly turned up at the end, and her thin lips--even without lipstick--are dark. Her complexion, even in the winter, is a light, all over olive. Her ink-black pubic bush, like I mentioned, is an overgrown and generally tangled thicket.

I don't mean it to sound like Vera is homely. She isn't. Vera actually has very pleasant facial features, and would probably be quite pretty---in a pixyish sort of way--if she took the trouble to fix herself up. But, with a husband like Ron, what would be use of doing it.

Ron stands maybe two inches taller than Vera does, but he outweighs her by close to a hundred pounds. Basically, Ron is your bland, non-descript, stubby-tubby, with wispy red hair and oversized geek glasses. Vera giggled like a schoolgirl when she overheard me describe her hubby in this way to someone else at a party.

Ron and Vera are both in their late thirties. They don't have any kids, and Ron's allergic to both dogs and cats. Ron is a crew foreman with the local Power Company; Vera's a stay-at-home housewife. Ron plays an up and down game of golf--generally down. Vera could play much better than she normally does. She's got the natural talent. When she doesn't think anyone is watching her, and she concentrates on what she's doing, her timing of the clubface meeting the ball is textbook perfection. She just doesn't have the confidence in herself to do it each and every time she picks up a club.

And that is probably Vera's only serious fault; she's her own worst enemy. At home, or around people she's known for a long time and is comfortable being with, she's okay. She can even exude a bubbly effervescence. But, on her own, Vera is an introverted wallflower, almost in the extreme at times. But, I like her, and I've always sensed that she really likes me. I'm Vera's best friend and she's told me things she's probably never revealed to anyone else, things she might otherwise not even admit to herself, so I know she's totally wrong concerning her self-image. Everyone who's met her likes Vera. They just wish she'd open up, let her hair down, kick off her shoes, and allow herself to have some fun.

Okay, now you, hopefully, have a clearer picture of four of the players in this. So, back to the story.

***

Vera called back twenty minutes later and confirmed that they were going with us. "Great," I told her. And I really meant it. I then debated with myself before asking, "What's this going to cost you, Vera?" I wasn't inquiring about monetarily. Ron made damned good money and could easily afford this trip.

"One of Ron's, quote, Private Moments." I could hear the distaste in her voice. "Thank God it'll only last about that long."

This, I find very sad. Ron and Vera have only been married six years longer than Randy and me, and their sex life is clearly dull and boring. It makes me wondered if there ever was any real spark to it.

"So," Vera bubbled in a much happier tone, "when do we leave?"

"Friday night. Now that we know how many are for sure going, Randy said he'll call and book seats for eight on the early flight. That'll put us in Loco Springs in time to catch the tail end of Happy Hour."

"Then, I'll be packed and waiting in the morning. See ya, Liz"

I laughed as I hung up. It was only Tuesday night. "Well, we are officially two full foursomes," I announced as I entered the study where Randy was playing chess against the computer.

"That's really great, Honey," he grumbled.

"Can it, Poophead. Ron's not that bad." I stood behind him and massaged his shoulders. "Look on the bright side, the way Ron plays, you and Greg should be able to take him to the cleaners in two or three days."

Randy tilted his head back and smiled up at me. "That is a much brighter prospect." He sat up and flexed his back muscles. "So, what would you like to do now?"

I walked over to the doorway, turned to look at him, and bluntly stated, "Get fucked," before sticking my tongue out at him and racing for the stairs.

And that is just exactly what I meant. Fucking is another way Randy and I have of warding off the debilitating effects of Cabin Fever. For me, it's the absolute best way.

Randy was upstairs, in his socks, with his shirt off and his unbuttoned, unzipped pants tangled around his muscular legs by the time I waltzed out of the bathroom--butt naked. I snootily looked him up and down. He sortta reminded me of my date on prom night; a severely horned-up high school boy on the verge of blowing his nuts before he even got his pants off. Of course, being a virgin at the time-- and an anxious to learn virgin at that, I'd had some fairly wet and aggravatingly twisted panties of my own to contend with in that cramped backseat on that hymen-fatal night.

I went around him to the bed, laid down, reached over and picked up the book I was currently reading. "Guess you're not that interested," I sniped as I opened the book and pretended to read.

With a lot of grunts and curses--which, believe me, were damned near impossible to keep from giggling at--Randy finally got naked then lunged onto the bed and slapped the book from my hands. "I hope you want this hard and fast, you snooty bitch," he growled. "Cause that's just how you're gonna get it."

With a bored sigh, I retrieved my book, put the bookmark back in the right place, and placed it back on the nightstand. Then, I glared up at him. "Not so fast, Caveman. First, I want you to fuck my mouth, and I do mean fuck it all the way."

Having scrupulously studied the movie of the same name back when I was in college, I had learned how to successfully Deep Throat a ten-inch vibrator. Therefore, taking all seven inches of Randy's hard cock down my throat was mere child's play. Okay, that would be considered practicing very nasty child's play, this country's most taboo illegality, which can get you twenty-five to life in most states. So, sue me for being a horny wifey who enjoys playing really nasty kid games with her hubby's big ol' cock.

And, speaking of cock... I reached down and took a firm hold on Randy's hard rod. "Then," I carefully instructed as I gave that sweet dick of his a not-so-gentle squeeze, "then I want you to ram this hard pole into my hot cunt and fuck me hard, and fast, and deep, till I go blewy...at least twice."

"And," he savagely demanded, "what about my needs?"

I smiled up at my husband, ever so sweetly. "Baby, if you haven't gone blewy yourself by then, I want to pull your cock out of me, scoot up against my tits, and shoot your hot juice right here." I opened my mouth wide and swirled my tongue around inside it. "I want you to cumm right straight into your loving wife's ever-ready loving cup."

No sooner had I finished putting in my salacious requests, then I was getting my ever-ready mouth stuffed with the swollen head of a very nice and very hard cock. I raised my head, allowing all seven inches of that cock to enter my mouth and slide on down my relaxed throat. Then, I clamped my lips tight around the base of his cock and laid my head back on the pillow, drawing Randy by his captured pecker along with me. With him now poised above me, I garbled, "Do it," around the pulsating cockhead lodged in my accommodating gullet.

And do it my Randy most certainly did. After a couple of tentative in and out fucks--to insure that my gag reflex wasn't going to kick in--he began to really feed me his cock, and I do mean feed it to me all the way. Sometimes I enjoy giving my husband nice, soft oral sex, but this wasn't one of those nice times. This night I wanted him to face-fuck me like a cheap, slutty whore. Believe it or not, I can cum from being deeply face-fucked.

And this night was no exception. Randy hit absolute bottom and a minor orgasm rippled through me, causing me to involuntarily swallow. Since swallowing around a cock in your throat tends to make most men cum right then and there, I yanked my mouth off Randy's cock the second I felt his testicles, being warmly held in the palm of my hand, begin to tighten up. "Put it in me, Baby," I urged as I shoved him back down between my anxiously elevated legs. "Ram it in there, Stud. Slam that hard cock all the way home and pound your wife's hot cunt till you make her go blewy."

When it comes to down and dirty fucking, ramming his hard cock all the way to the hilt in my pussy and then fucking me plumb senseless, Randy is the best at doing it that I've ever known. If I ever came across someone who could do me better than Randy, I knew I would be in danger of becoming a complete and hopeless sex maniac.

Randy slapped the ol' to meat me hard and fast and I, indeed, went blewy. But, I had insisted on going blewy at least twice, and Bard was determined to see to it that I did, so he didn't let up. Thank God! He fucked me straight into a second blewy, then a third, and even stronger orgasm, which, I swear, actually slammed up against the second. I came so hard, I felt like a leaf caught in the eye of a hurricane, whirling out of control, being buffeted back and forth by high winds whenever I came too close to the storm itself. Goddamn, it was great.

It became impossible for me to keep my legs in the air any longer. "Pull out, Honey," I wheezed as my heels hit the bed. "Bring that big, bad cock of yours up here and give it to me right in the mouth."

Randy pulled out and slid up my body until he was actually sitting on my tits, his one-eyed monster staring me right in the ol' kisser. I took it--all slick and glistening with my juices--in both of my hands and crammed its dribbling head into my eager mouth. I let him slide his whole cock in and out through my hands, across and around my swirling tongue, and down my throat until I felt his balls tighten against my chin. The next time he pulled back, I stopped his inward thrust and clamped my lips tight around the head of his cock. I then furiously jacked him off.

In just a couple of seconds, a hard jet of hot cum hit the roof of my mouth. Luckily, I had closed off my throat with the back of my tongue, just in the nick of time. Three more hard jets filled my mouth, then a weaker forth, but I kept on jacking and sucking until no more of his cum was going seep out, or could be forcibly sucked out of that sweet-spitting one-eyed monster my husband has between his legs.

Satisfied that I had accomplished my cock-sucking mission, I let his slimy cock slip from between my cum-slick lips. I swirled the salty/sweet cum around in my mouth a few times before winking at him and opening my mouth wide. I made sure he got a good look at his wife's mouth filled with her husband's slimy, yummie cum, and then I swallowed it all down.

"Liz," Randy shook his head with wonderment "you can be such a nasty slut sometimes."

"Thanks for the compliment." I smiled and pulled him down, and kissed him full on the mouth. "And thank you for being the absolute best nasty-slut-fucker I know."

"I love you, Liz."

"And I love you, too, Caveman."

Randy had to be in early the following morning, so we put any more nasty games I might come up with on the shelf for the night and cuddled till we both drifted off to sleep. But, at the end of the week, we were going to be winging our way south, to Loco Springs, Nevada where there was plenty of warm yellow sun and green greens...for a whole week. And, just because we were going to be out of the cold and snow, there was no reason for us to suspend our kooky, kinky ways of dealing with Cabin Fever boredom.

It was too bad Vera's sorry sex life probably wasn't going to perk up while we were down there. I wished there were something I could do about it, even if it was just holding her hand and telling her it was going to be okay... someday.

Only, in my dream, it wasn't Vera's hand I was holding. My hand was tangled in an ink black bramble bush. It was seeking out a hidden pleasure cave. My hand instinctively knew that elusive cavern had to be in there, somewhere, just waiting for my searching fingers to locate it, and then swiftly enter its mysterious, cream-filled confines.

Oh, did I forget to mention that your storyteller tends to have kinky and vividly explicit dreams? And in living color, too.

Part 2

It figured! An hour before we were to board the flight to Loco Springs, Barb calls and says her babysitter is snowed in and can't get out. But, Mr. Thorne has a way of solving the problem and that we should go on ahead and the four of them would take a later flight.

Praying that this Mr. Thorne would make good on his promise, Brad, Ron, Vera and I went ahead and boarded the plane. The flight itself was bumpy, but otherwise uneventful, as most commuter flights generally are. No one tried to hijack the flight to somewhere else or anything like that. The plane being half filled with golfers, anxious to get out of the dreadful winter and enjoy chasing a ball around green hills for a few days, the poor guy would have been severely bludgeoned with a multitude of 9, 8, and 7 irons, led by Vera, angrily wielding her mallet-head putter.

The rented car Brad had arraigned for was waiting for us and we drove to the hotel. We checked in and agreed to meet in the lounge ...as soon as we had all gone potty... to wait for Barb, Greg, and the Thornes to, hopefully, arrive.

You can imagine our surprise when we entered the lounge and found Barb, Greg, and an interracial couple sitting there, calmly having drinks. "How the hell...?" I gaped at Barb with total disbelief.

Barb grinned up at me. "Deek and Darcy," she said, nodding at the good-looking black man sitting across from her. "Derrick owns a construction company. He had six front loaders plow a road right up to Julie's front door, with him and Greg following behind in his Durango. Meanwhile, Darcy calls and charters a private jet. The guys dropped Julie off at the house and met the two of us at the airport and away we went." Her aggravating grin broadened. "Didn't you see Darcy and I waving to you as our little jet went past your prop job like it was standing still?"

My eyes flicked to Derrick Thorne. "Her story," he said, throwing up his hands. "All I did was drive the $35,000 snowmobile."

"And all I did was make a phone call," the stunning strawberry blonde sitting beside Barb chimed in. "All I did was ride shotgun," Greg cheerfully added.

I threw up my own hands. "If this is any indication of things to come," I said with a beaming smile, "then God help Loco Springs this week."

Another table was slid in alongside theirs as introductions were made all around and I ended up seated beside Derrick. I'm not a short person, but I still had to look up to see his face. Even sitting down he was an imposing figure. Large, without showing any fat, with dark, laughing eyes, brilliant white teeth, huge black paws for hands, and no dreadlocks or cornrows in his short-cropped ink black hair. And, God, he was distressingly handsome.

"Don't let it intimidate you, Elizabeth," he said with a disarming smile. "I'm just a big cuddly teddy bear, really."

"Yeah, a two hundred and twenty pound teddy bear," Darcy snorted then smiled. "But really cuddly."

I looked her way. Like I already mentioned, she was a stunning strawberry. Along with that pale-reddish flaxen hair of hers went the epitome of a peaches and cream complexion, complement by sparkling, intelligent, sea green eyes. And, resting on her crossed arms on top of the table, I honestly must admit, was a healthy set of breasts underneath her pink polo shirt.

I pulled my eyes away from Darcy and held out (slightly up, actually) my hand to Derrick. "It's Liz, among friends."

His big black paw engulfed my hand. "Deek, to friends."

Our drinks arrived and Deek told a couple of stories about playing pro ball, mostly for the guy's benefit, but I enjoyed hearing them, too. I'm another rarity among women; a devoted pro football nut.

A lulled ensued and then Darcy proceeded to entertain not only our joined tables, but also any table within the sound of her musical voice. She wasn't just witty, she was absolutely hilarious. Cracking jokes and telling stories ...some ribald, but most just down right funny. Darcy was showstopper, bar none. Put her on stage and slap a microphone in her hands, and stunning Darcy Thorne could have made some serious money as a standup comedian.

As entertaining as Darcy was, I found myself conversing more with Deek. He had a sharp intellect, he was perceptively astute, and he was captivatingly articulate. (As well as being deceptively soft spoken for such a big man.) He might have been a wide receiver's worst nightmare out on the field (or so his reputation had been), but here, out of a combat situation, he was utterly charming. I liked him immediately.

We somehow got on the topic of motivation. "Greed is the motivating factor in most human decisions," he explained to me. "Could be an insatiable greed for wealth, or power, even sex. Find out what a person's motivating factor is and you can control their actions, as well as their reactions, to almost any situation."

"Sounds like mind control to me," I ventured.

"No. You can never buy another person's loyalty, just control their responses with proper stimuli." Deek glanced across the room. "Take that waitress over there. I've been watching her since we arrived and I know exactly what her primary motivation is." He reached in his pocket and tossed a money clip... with a wad of bills big enough to choke a horse, right on the table. "It's money, Liz."

She was a very pretty young woman with a great figure, the kind of overly buxom shape, perkiness, and girl-next-door looks men find irresistible. "I'm sure there are other things that motivate her."

"Only after the almighty dollar," he countered. "I'll prove it to you." Deek caught her eye and motioned her over. When she got to our table he said, "I'll have what that man you just served is drinking."

"Club soda with a twist of lime," she replied with a 'tip-me-generously' smile and started to turn away.

"No, Miss, I think you've misunderstood my request. I said I'd have what that man is drinking." The girl looked down at him quizzically and Deek picked up the money clip. "How much would it take for you to go back over there, take the drink from that man's hand, bring it back over here, and set it in front of me?"

"Are you kidding, Mister?" she laughed. "Something like that could cost me my job."

Before the girl could respond further, Deek peeled a crisp hundred dollar bill off his wad and laid it on the table, then he quickly upped the ante to two one hundred dollar bills. The girl's eyes went wide and after a few seconds, Deek added a third hundred dollar bill. The girl's eyes went even wider and Deek put another hundred on the growing stack of bills. The waitress's amazed eyes flashed to the customer in question, then to where the bartender was located at the far end of the bar, then back down at the four hundred dollars. Never once did she look directly at Deek.

With an exaggerated sigh, Deek put a fifth hundred on top then concealed the reward with his huge hand. "Last offer, Miss."

Without a word, the waitress turned around, marched over to the other table, took the drink right out of the startled guy's hand, brought it back to our table, set it down right in front of Deek, and held out her hand.

With that award winning smile of his, Deek put the bills in her hand then gently folded it around the money. "You can take the drink back to the gentleman, Miss." He winked at her. "And please inform the table that their tab for the night is being put on mine."

The girl shook her head. "Mister, you're nutso."

"There you have it, Liz," Deek said as the girl left to give the guy his drink back, "I didn't buy her loyalty, just her cooperation in a little experiment."

This was one man I would not want sitting across a poker table from me. And, any business dealings I might have with Derrick Thorne would, most assuredly, be attended by a "Dream Team" of financial analysts, and probably a couple of top criminal lawyers, thrown in for good measure, as well.

Darcy scowled across the table at Deek. "What did it cost you this time?"

"The five hundred I gave the waitress, plus whatever their table's tab is going to be for the night."

"Not too bad... this time," Darcy said with a smirk. "Seen nights it cost you lot more to play the outrageous Nigger."

"It's a cultural perception thing, Liz," Deek said out of the side of his mouth. "If a black athlete doesn't do something totally outrageous every now and again, people think he's trying to be white."

Darcy stood up and in a voice loud enough to be heard several tables away, announced, "All right, you big, ugly, black ape, it's about time you carted my white ass upstairs and fucked me senseless."

"Yes, Ma'am," Deek said with a lopsided grin. And you could have heard a pin drop on the carpeted floor as he got up, went around the table, picked her up and slung her over his broad shoulder like a sack of tatters, and headed out of the lounge.

At the entry, Darcy threw out her hands and grabbed the door jamb, stopping them from proceeding any farther. "It's okay, folks," she laughed, "we're married... rings and everything. Honest."

She squealed and let go of the jams when Deek slapped her on the ass and told her to behave herself. "At least in public."

Laughing myself, I looked around the table. The guys were sitting there with their mouths open. Vera was chuckling. It was Barb who was having the most fun. Actually, I was a bit concerned that she might wet herself, she was laughing so hard.

Oh, I liked the Thornes. They were going to be a fun couple, Deek with his wit, intelligence, and his penetrating perception of human behavior, not to mention his charming, good looks, and Darcy with her irreverent sense of propriety. This was going to be an enjoyable week, whether I had even one good game, or not.

With the Thornes having retired to see to Darcy's sensible fucking, the party broke up. And, as Brad and I and Barb and Greg headed upstairs to see what could be done about some totally senseless fucking of our own, Vera headed off in the direction of the nearest slot machine, a full bucket of quarters firmly in hand. Ron went upstairs alone.

***

"So," I inquired as I slipped my dress over my head and kicked off my heels, "what do you think of the Thornes?"

"Darcy's funny," Brad answered, trying to get both his slacks and briefs off over his shoes. "Sharp, too. She might be strawberry blonde on top, but that's where the blonde ends and the brains begin." His slacks, briefs and shoes in a heap at the foot of the bed, he launched himself into the middle of our impending playground. "Did you know she graduated from UNLV, with a 3.8 5 GPA?"

"Not till just now." I unsnapped my bra and casually let it drop. "And Deek?"

"Derrick seems like a good egg. I saw him play when he was with the pros. He was one helluva DB." Brad's no racist, but I couldn't help picking up on how he'd used Derrick instead of Deek. Brad had played ball in college, and had been a pretty good running back, but he hadn't tried to turn pro, so maybe it was a little athletic jealousy. "Derrick's no dumb jock, either," Brad continued while he impatiently waited for me to finish undressing and join him on the bed. "The way he parlayed that multi-million dollar contract Dallas gave him into his "affluent" living took some real smarts."

I skinned off my panties and looked up. Brad's rock-hard cock was pointing skyward, like a guided

167

missile on the launching pad; a quivering penile missile I didn't want going off just yet. So, seductively attired in just my garter belt and nylons, I remained standing at the foot of the bed. "How do you think he'll do with you guys tomorrow?"

"We'll see. He was a hot-shot jock and all, but picking off an errant pigskin is a whole lot easier than hitting a golf ball." Brad grabbed his cock and menacingly shook it at me. "A little white ball that's probably half as big as the head of his black dick."

"Hummmm?" I hummed inside my head, as I snake-slid onto the bed. I swiped Brad's cock from his hand, kissed the head of it, then took the entire thing into my mouth and down my throat in one felled swoop, and proceeded to give him one of my "killer" blowjobs.

Why, you ask? Why had I hummed inside my head, and why, when I had wanted to prolong things just a little, had I immediately swallowed my husband's entire cock...something I knew would guarantee his shooting off fairly quick? Well, I know it's not politically correct, and that it's stereotyping in the extreme, but the thought of the bulbous head of Deek's black cock being twice the size of a golf ball, I must admit, made for one helluva stimulating mental image with which to help launch a ready to-go-explode penis missile.

And did my husband's nasty slut make that hard, throbbing penile missile of his launch a load of hot cum? Wow! Did I ever. And dead on target, too. Meaning, right down my swallowing throat and into my anxiously waiting belly. "Yuuuummmie!"

My dreams that night revolved around me chasing this mysterious, over-sized black golf ball all over a pristine white course and every time we ended up on the green together, the putt I would have to make would invariably be longer and more difficult than any I had ever tried to sink. Yet, every one of those impossible putts ran straight and true, as if the cup was base metal and the ball magnetized.

I should have been ecstatic, but I wasn't, because the cup was not exactly the gooey hole on that lily-white mattress I wanted to hear that mesmerizing big black ball going plop inside.

Part 3

The guys, as expected were up and gone before daybreak. I stayed in bed until six-thirty, then got up, showered, and went down to the coffee shoppe for some much-needed caffeine. Darcy was already there. "You always sleep this late?" she jabbed playfully.

"Caffeine first," I growled back. "Then we can fence."

My life-saving coffee arrived along with Vera, and Darcy asked her, "You as grumpy as sour puss here before you get some coffee?"

Vera smiled. "Not quite as much."

Barb stumbled in as Vera's coffee was being set on the table. "So," she asked, swiping Vera's cup, "how much did you lose before following Ron upstairs?"

"Only one bucket," Vera answered matter-of-factly.

"Better pace yourself better than that, Quarter Lady. We're supposed to be here a full week, and..."

"I will. And, speaking of pacing..." Standing up and snatching all the loose quarters off the table, Vera was on her way to the slots.

Barb shook her head. "If her libido was as powerful as her gambling urge, Ron would be in intensive care on a regular basis."

"Maybe it is," Darcy ventured. "Maybe in private, Vera's a sexual tigress."

"Yeah, right," I snorted. "Vera thinks a pussy's mostly for peeing purposes."

"Ohhh, shit," Barb groaned and quickly got up. "Why did you have to mention peeing?"

"Why didn't you take care of that upstairs?" I asked.

"I did." Barb scowled down at me. "Just wait till you have a kid and see how it fucks up your plumbing." Darcy and I both snickered as Barb headed off in search of the nearest ladies room.

"Well," Darcy said when we were finally alone again, "are you going to ask, or not?"

"Ask what?"

"The question you've been wanting to ask me since last night. Admit it, Liz, you want to know what it's like to make love with a black man."

"No I don't," I responded defensively. "Not... not really." Not really, my ever lovin' ass. I was dying to know what it was like.

"Sure you do, and I don't mind you asking. Honest. Cross my heart, and I promise to spit the instant we get outside." Darcy was smiling at the time-honored oath she had just made to me, but her luminous green eyes weren't joking. "Liz, if I don't asked get that sort of question from at least ten white women a month, I always get the questioning looks: What's it feel like to have a big, black cock in your pussy? What's it like to have one in your mouth? Are black cocks really bigger then white cocks? Does a black man's cum taste different then a white man's? Do they truly cum more than white men? Does he call you his white slut bitch?"

"All right," I admitted, "so maybe I am a little curious. I mean, switch places and you'd probably be wondering the same thing about me."

"I would," Darcy affirmed with an additional nod of her pretty head. She took a sip of her coffee and contemplatively set the cup back down. "The problem is, I can't give you an answer, not a definitive one, anyway."

"And why not?"

"Because, never having had a white cock in me, I've got no solid basis for making a fair and unbiased comparison."

My eyes narrowed. "That sounded an awful lot like lawyer-ease?"

"It should. I majored in Corporate Law at UNLV."

That figured. Brad had said she was sharp. "You've never been with a white man?" I asked. "Not even once?"

"Not even one. I knew early on what I liked--on the night of my fourteenth birthday, actually, and I never saw any reason to go shopping on the other side of the fence for a different flavor." Darcy smiled. "So to speak."

"Then you've always preferred ah... chocolate to vanilla." It was my turn to smile. "So to speak."

"Yep."

Barb returned, took one look at me, and turned to Darcy. "What have you two been talking about that's got her cheeks all blushing pink? Sex, I'll bet."

"Sort of. Liz just admitted to wondering what it was like to make love to a black man."

"It's pretty much the same as with a white guy," Barb said to me. "And different, too."

"You've done it?" I asked.

"Couple of times. Back in my wild and carefree college days. But, not Since then."

"Then you'd be the better one to answer her questions."

Barb cocked her head at Darcy. "How so?"

"Darcy's never been with a white man," I answered.

Barb's eyes went wide. "Never?"

Darcy shook her head. "Nope!"

"Humph!" Barb got an evil look in her eyes. "You know, Darcy, I think Liz really ought to find out something like that for herself."

Darcy nodded her agreement. "Actual, hands-on experience really is the best teacher."

Vera, her hands now empty of quarters, reappeared at the table. "The best teacher of what?" she asked.

"Of finding out what being with a black man is like," Barb answered.

"But, surely Darcy could tell her. At least a little bit."

"Nope," I said.

"For the third time," Darcy said with a weary sigh, "I've never been with a white man."

"Imagine that," Vera mused, taking her seat. She signaled a nearby waitress for another round of coffees and turned to Barb. "So tell me, what's all this about Liz learning hands-on with a hard, black penis?"

"Just girl jabbing, Vera." Only, something in the sound of Barb's voice sounded an awful lot like she wished it wasn't just harmless jabbing.

Out of the blue, "It ah... it doesn't have to be," Darcy offered. "I mean, if you're ah... if you're really that interested, Liz, it could be arranged. Discretely, of course."

"I don't think I'm that curious, Darcy," I responded quickly. "Not even if it was arranged discretely. But, thanks anyway for the offer."

"How?" Barb blurted out. "With..."

"No, not with Deek," Darcy said with a no-nonsense shake of her head. "Sorry, girls, but that big, handsome black hunk is all mine."

"Then, with who?" Barb persisted.

"With whom," Darcy corrected. "I've got a... a friend in Las Vegas who would set it up for me, a clean hotel room and a nice guy, not some coked-up junkie off the street."

"Really?" Vera asked.

"One phone call and it's a done deal."

"Do it," Barb urged her.

"Yes," Vera quickly added. "Make the phone call, Darcy."

"Now just hold on here," I croaked, "I haven't agreed to anything, and you three already have me in Vegas with a black dick aimed at my defenseless white pussy."

"Actually, it's dark brown," Vera pointed out. "And very nicely groomed, too."

"Why not, Liz?" Barb demanded. "You're the one always saying how she's not afraid to experiment. How a little taste of the forbidden always makes you so wet."

"Right," Vera enthusiastically joined in. "I've heard you say that, too. And Darcy said it would be clean, with a nice guy. And she promises to see that it would be done discretely."

"But," I protested, "I'm... I'm married."

"So are the rest of us, Liz," Barb hammered. "And we're not about to spill the beans if one of us gets lucky."

This was not going the way I had wanted. All I had wanted to find out was what being with a black man was like, not that I wanted to try it for myself.

Oh, hell! Who am I kidding here? I wanted to try a black cock for myself in the worst way, and Darcy had just handed me one on a silver platter. So to speak.

"Come on, Liz, do it." Barb could tell I was weakening. "Tell you what, if you will, so will I. And... and right in front of you, too, so you'll know I'm not pulling a fast one on ya."

"So will I," Vera surprisingly added.

Darcy almost spilled her coffee. "You, too?"

"Sure. Why not? I don't see why Liz and Barb should get to have all the fun." Vera's tone became indignantly defensive. "I have fantasies, too, you know."

I hesitated. I hemmed and I hawed. I fought inside my head with my growing urge for a taste of the unknown. Finally, I agreed. "All right, but if either of you reneges, I swear I'll rip her fucking pubic hairs out. One FUCKING hair at a time!"

Over breakfast, the sneaky, underhanded plans for my (and Barb's, and Vera's, too) black debauchery were laid. Up front, Darcy made it clear that she wouldn't be involved. She would get it set up for us, and she'd stay around to help anyway she could, but she wouldn't indulge herself with the guy. Deek was all the man she needed, or wanted.

Once we had everything satisfactorily hashed out, our nefarious scheme's final version was presented to the guys over a late lunch. They could have the rooms, the big beds, and the surrounding golf courses all to themselves for the next couple of days, we girls were heading for Vegas for a "girls only" gambling and golf junket. And, also, since we were so close, so that Darcy could visit with an old friend who lived there.

Ron's response was a vague, "Sure. Go ahead."

Brad and Greg took a little longer to consider things, but they eventually agreed with good ol' non-committal Ron.

Derrick eyed Darcy for a long moment before saying, "Why not. You and Tracy haven't seen each other in a year or so. Besides, it'll give me a couple of days to properly pluck these sorry pigeons."

"You got the bucks this morning only because I underestimated you, jock." Brad's tone was threatening, but not serious. "Next time out, your black ass is gonna be all mine."

"Trash talk!" Deek gleefully yelped. He raised his big paw in the air and signaled for another round of drinks. He winked at Darcy and smiled broadly at

Brad. "You mus' be dreamin' inside yo fool head...
white boy."

There was no animosity in this exchange. It was
just what Deek had called it; trash talk between two
athletes who had developed a healthy respect for
each other.

Greg turned to Ron. "If we end up paired
against them, I'm handing over my half at the first
tee and slinking off, with my tail between my legs,
for the driving range."

Ron grinned weakly. "And I'll already be there,
waitin' for ya, Buddy."

Brad and Deek just grinned across the table at
each other. Kinda like a pair of territorial apes, high
on their own testosterone.

Darcy went to place the call to her friend, Barb
went in search of a potty, Vera trotted off with
another bucket of quarters, and I sat back with my
drink to mull this whole thing over.

Ok, the guys had bought our--to my mind--
pretty lame excuse. So far, so good. But, how good
was what they hadn't been let in on going to be
where I was concerned? I would be cheating on
Brad for the first time since we had gotten married,
and with a black man, no less. Not that Brad or I
have anything against interracial mixing. We've
known a number of interracial couples and have
enjoyed many nights out the town with them and
none too few backyard barbecues, either. And
weren't we all getting along just famously with the
Thorne's?

Well, Ron might not be having a whale of a good time, but who gave a rat's ass whether that spineless worm was having a good time. Vera clearly wanted to spend as little time as she had to with her husband, and I got the distinct impression that Ron would just as soon be back up in the frozen north, or at least not have his wife down here with him.

Anyway, in a purely psychological sense, I figured I could handle the cheating side of what I was about to do, even with the interracial aspect thrown in, or so I fervently hoped. Physically, however, if all the exaggerated rumors I had ever heard about black men and their overly developed pricks were indeed true, I could be in for some trouble. Brad's seven inches filled me up quite nicely, but just how wide open could a pussy be stretched... comfortably? 'We'll all just have wait and see', I told myself. 'Wouldn't I'?

As for my two willing accomplices? Barb, with her big mouth, I figured was on her own. She said she had been down this black tar road before, so she knew what she was in for.

Vera, though... If the guy Darcy's friend lined up for us had more than in the penis department the pitiful pickle she had once told me Ron possessed, with Vera's waifish build, her harmless black fantasy could turn out to be real trouble for her. Serious! Painful! Trouble!

Whatever, in a matter of hours, we'd all three be finding out the dark truth. We'd all three be getting what we asked for; hard, black cock, maybe even a lot more black cock than any of us was bargaining for. Provided, of course, that the guy Darcy's friend set us up with was up to handling three horny white lady's black fantasies.

It could even happen that one of us might not get enough hard, spurting, black cock. I thought it was unlikely that this would occur. But, as they say, anything's possible.

That's not to say it was probable. Though closely related, the two are vastly different. Possible means it could happen, probable that there is a good likelihood of it happening. And there, dear reader, is your pompous grammar lesson for the day.

A worse scenario would be if one of us became obsessed with black men, that she not only wouldn't get enough black cock, but that she couldn't get enough. That she, in effect, became addicted to the stark contrasts intrinsic to interracial sex. This I couldn't even imagine happening, not from the three of us. Even still, within some of the darker recesses I've had to delve into doing legal research, I've learned that even the unthinkable is not only possible, but is all too often carried out by minds much sicker than even the infamous Hannibal Lecter's.

But, say that scenario was to take place. Which one of us three could become that insatiable, black-cock-craving, white slut? Vera? No. Vera was not a likely candidate. She was entirely too much of an introvert. She was too meek and insecure, especially about her body. Despite all that, Vera was not a sexual being. Although, she had become more than mildly indignant when she thought she might be excluded from realizing a black fantasy.

Maybe it would be Barb; a far more likely prospect for this possibility. She said she had been there before, and we've all heard the adage: Once you go black, you'll never come back. Case in point; our new friend, Darcy Thorne. No, Darcy had been initiated with interracial sex and had never experienced sex with a white man. She couldn't go back to something she had never known. For Darcy, that would be crossing the color line, in reverse.

I scratched Barb off the short list. One time Grammar School teacher, now stay-at-home mommy, Barbara might be willing to trifle on the other side of the color line, but to obsessively immerse herself in the pleasures of black on white sex, no. Socially conscious Barb wouldn't do anything that might jeopardize her secure, upper income, country club existence.

That left only...? Good, Lord! That left only insatiably horny and sexually experimental Moi. Could something like that actually happen to me? Could I get one taste of what Darcy referred to as "Hot Chocolate" and become so totally addicted that I might end up excluding Brad from my sex life?

God, I sure as hoped it couldn't. The way I loved that ol' Poophead/Caveman of mine, so hard, and so passionately...

I yanked my downward spiraling thoughts back into the realm of reality. For shit sake, all we were doing was sneaking off to Vegas to satisfy our ah...

our natural curiosity. How bad a thing could that be? Realistically, what was the worst that could happen; that one of us might get a bigger cock than we could handle and end up walking a little funny for a couple of days, maybe not be able to pee without it stinging for a day or two? Hell, that could be explained away as a pulled muscle or a minor yeast infection.

Darcy said her friend would see to it that everything was nice and clean, and that it would be handled with the utmost discretion. And I trusted Darcy. Why, I wasn't sure. I had only known her for less than twenty-four hours, yet something that came from inside her told me that Darcy Thorne would never intentionally do anything that might bring harm or disrepute to someone she was close to. And the four of us gals were close. Barb, Vera and I hadn't become tight with Darcy as yet, but that would come, eventually. Of this, I was certain. Don't ask me how I knew this, I just did. Okay?

And don't ask me when I first realized that the four of us were becoming friends, either. If I had to hazard a guess, I would say it had been over our subversive breakfast. As we had been hashing out the details of this salacious sojourn of ours into finding out, first hand, what black on white sex was really like, plotting and scheming how we were going to pull it off, we had, in effect, been the Three Lady Musketeers with our female D'Artagnan.

I could trust Darcy Thorne, we all could. Of this I was dead certain, and there's no more of a certainty than death. Well, is there?

Still and all, I guess anything is possible these days.

Part 4

We were an hour out of Loco Springs, cruising down I66 in a white Cadillac convertible at seventy miles per hour, the top down, Darcy behind the wheel, when Barb suggested a little, "Truth or Dare".

Being naturally inquisitive, ("Nosey is more like it.") it's Barb's favorite party game. Not mine. "Darcy's going to be severely handicapped as far as dares go," I forlornly pointed out from the back seat, hoping the tone in my voice would dissuade her from persisting, yet knowing it wouldn't.

"Then she'll just have to opt for the truth," Barb retaliated. "Who goes first?"

"Your game, you should go first," Darcy quickly said, buying herself a little time before she got asked anything too incriminating. "Lay a good one on her, Liz."

'Way to go, Darcy', I mentally congratulated her as Barb frowned across the front seat. Barb didn't like going first. Being the last one tagged gave her the opportunity to see just how probing the questions would be. Well, it was about time she got her nosey comeuppance. "Okay, Barb, you said you had done what we're headed off to do; how about telling all of us when, with whom, and how it was?"

"That's a three-parter, Damnit!" Barb protested.

"You never laid down any rules first," Vera surprisingly challenged. "Now, answer up, or I'll lay real nasty a dare on your sorry ass."

Wallflower Vera hated this silly game more than I did, and for her to join in so readily was way out of character. But, I had noticed that, ever since leaving Loco Springs, Vera's normally listless brown eyes had taken on a dreamy sort of glimmer, as if she was truly looking forward to whatever lay ahead for us in Vegas. 'Could Vera be the one of us who...?'

"Vera's right," Darcy said. Over our conniving breakfast, she had been assimilated into our little clique and instinctively knew how the game was played; if no rules had been laid down beforehand, you made your own. "And if Vera can't come up with something real nasty," she quickly added, "I'm sure Liz or I can."

Oh, yes, I was liking wicked witch Darcy Thorne more and more.

Barb was now caught in a three-pronged attack, and as stubborn as she can be, retreating was out of the question. "Okay, it was my sophomore year... the first time. I was at a frat party, dancing with this black guy... I'd had way too much tequila... the guy was nice looking... he had this impossible bulge in his pants I just had to see in the flesh to believe it was for real. Anyway, we eventually danced our way up to one of the dorm rooms, got naked, and... And it was for real, all right. It wasn't all the way hard yet and was still the biggest cock I had ever seen."

Barb stopped talking and her eyes went misty with memory. Only Vera's insistent voice brought her back from her reverie. "That's the when and almost the who. Now make with the how was it."

"Unbelievable," Barb answered in a throaty whisper. "Un-Fucking-believable. Once I got my hand around it, I didn't want to ever let go. It was so hard... and so hot. Even when it swelled to the point I couldn't close my fist around it, I still wouldn't let go. I sucked and jerked him off till he flooded my mouth with hot jizz, then continued to fondle that big black cock of his long after it had withered back to near normalcy. Even when he fucked me later on, I'm sure I could have taken all of it, but I just had to have at least some of that big, black pole of pleasure in my hand."

I was a little stunned. Barb and I had traded intimacies before, but she had never been quite this open with me, never before had quite the same sexual excitement been so evident in her voice.

Darcy was laughing. "Been there, Barb. And got a couple of stained T-shirts to prove it."

Vera's reaction to Barb's recounting of her first interracial experience was a different matter. It was one I never would have suspected from a retiring wallflower. She was slouched down in the seat, her head was laid back, her eyes were scrunched tight, and I had to look twice just to make double-damned certain I had seen what I thought I had seen. Vera's hand was shoved down inside her shorts, and it was busy. Very busy, indeed.

I caught Barb's eye and nodded over at Vera. She turned her head and her jaw dropped. "Vera, are you... are you masturbating?"

"Yes, damnit!" Vera snapped back. "And don't you dare tell me you don't do it, too, Barbara." Her eyes didn't open, nor did her hand stop moving inside her shorts. "You either, Liz."

"I do," I admitted. "And I sure Barb does, too." I could now smell Vera's heat. "We've just never considered being so public in our ah... our private moments." Vera's arousal was becoming a cloying atmosphere in the backseat, even with the top down. It was also stimulating. "Least, I haven't yet."

"Not until now," Barb wheezed.

I knew the smell of Vera's masturbating couldn't possibly reach beyond the back seat where Vera and I were, but the liquid squishing as her hand working on her pussy made it wetter and wetter could now be heard over the rushing wind. And it was clearly effecting Barb. Effecting her seriously.

With a low moan, Barb undid her seatbelt and knelt backwards on the front seat. Her hand disappeared down between her body and the back of the seat. I heard her unzip her golf shorts. She leaned over the back of the seat until her face was nearly in Vera's lap. "Show me, Vera," she demanded excitedly. "Let me see what you're doing to yourself."

Vera's eyes opened slowly, like she was forcing herself to waken from a deep sleep. Only, they weren't Vera's eyes anymore, not like I had ever seen them. Now they were on fire, intense, blazing with a look I had never seen in them before; the unmistakable look of lust... overheated animal lust.

Vera was in heat and nothing was going to detour her from satisfying her animalistic craving. Not Barb watching her masturbate, or me, not anything.

The most decadently wanton expression I've ever seen on another woman face spread across Vera's features and with her free hand she unbuttoned and unzipped her shorts. She lifted her ass off the seat and tugged and wiggled until she had pushed both her shorts and the white cotton panties she was wearing down past her knees. She bowed her freed knees out, and before Barb's enraptured eyes, she convincingly showed the both of us just exactly what she was doing to herself.

I glanced down at the wad of clothing bunched around Vera's exposed calves. The crotch of her panties was drenched. My eyes involuntarily came back up to between her legs. Vera's thick, tangled pubic hair was matted and glistened with her juice. Three of her fingers were buried in her cunt and as I enviously watched her masturbate, they began working even faster, ever deeper. And, the car rental agency wasn't going to be terribly pleased when they discovered the growing wet spot underneath Vera's ass and plunging fingers.

Vera's ass suddenly lurched off the seat and she yelped loudly. She had just made herself cum, no doubt of that. But, she didn't stop, she continued to unabashedly masturbate with an almost demonic determination. With a sharp intake of breath, Barb's eyes rolled back in their sockets. She had cum, too.

The two of them hearing and imagining Barb, actually being able to see Vera play. Both of them were masturbating and cuming. It was too much for me. I was wearing a golf skirt and panties, so it was easier for me to get to my yearning pussy. With a savage yank of my panties to one side, two, then three fingers were being crammed into my juicy cunt. It didn't take long and when Barb and Vera both came simultaneously, I made it a howling, spewing threesome.

With an anguished groan, Darcy applied the brakes, pulled off the road into a rest area, sped to the very back of it, and came to a screeching stop. "Damn you, Vera!" she cursed as she fumbled with her shorts and panties. "Damn the three of you all to hel... Ohhh, OOOOOOooooooo HHHHHH EEEEEEEEEEE LLLLLLLLLL... !!!!!"

An instant later, we became the four "cuming" Musketeers.

***

After the four of us had sheepishly cleaned ourselves up in the ladies room of the rest area, I sternly requested, "No more Truth or Dare, Barb," as Vera and I did our best to clean up the messes we had made in the back seat with wet clothes.

"Never again," Barb assured all of us as she and Darcy were doing the same thing to the front seat. She raised her head over the back of the seat and winked at me. "At least, not in public."

Back out on the road, I asked Vera what the hell had come over her. I didn't need to ask what had come over the rest of us. It had been the heat of the moment, as well as the wet heat between our legs. But, I did want to know what had made Vera

188

cast off her wallflower personality in favor of a wanton slut. Not only that, but to have cast it away so easily and so shamelessly.

"I masturbate all the time, Liz," she confessed without a shred of embarrassment. There was a glow to Vera that did absolute wonders for her. She was loose as the proverbial goose now and could at last be the person who hid inside of her. "I'll do it four, five, six times a day. Sometimes more. And then I'll get myself off in the bathroom or the family room maybe a dozen more times after Ron goes to bed."

I didn't know what to say to this revelation, so I kept my mouth shut and let Vera continue on her own.

"When you, or Ron, aren't around, I live in a fantasy world. Lots of wicked, nasty things go on there. Lots of lewd and lascivious things are done to me and for me there. I control what's done, how it's done, how much of it is done. Sometimes I just let it all go and have no control at all of what's happening to me." She smiled. "Those are the best orgasms of all, when I'm totally out of control."

"Lots of things happen in your fantasies, huh?" Barb inquired. "Like what, for instance?"

"Oh, everything, and anything," Vera replied. "Different men, multiple men alone with me. black men That comes around to visit me a lot lately. Women... I've even fantasize me having, shall we say, out of species sex when I'm really horny." She looked at me, her eyes challenging, yet seeming to ask forgiveness at the same time. "I guess that's why, when Barb was recounting her story, I just had to do what I did. I couldn't help it and I could stop once I started. If I shocked you, I'm sorry. But, I'm not apologizing."

"You don't have to," I told her. "If anyone should be apologizing, it's the three of us for interrupting by joining you."

"I'm glad you did, Liz. I'm glad all three of you joined me." Vera's much brighter eyes lowered, almost coquettishly. "It made what I was doing, what I was thinking about, that much hotter."

The rest of our exploratory road trip was fairly quiet. For me, it was contemplative. Something had happened here, a button had gotten pushed, a switch thrown, a trigger had been pulled inside Vera. Whatever, she was no longer the person I had known for a number of years. The free spirit that had secretly dwelled deep within her had been released and I wondered if the wallflower would ever reemerge. Could Vera ever again go back to who she had once been? Would I continue to see her this content with life, and with herself?

I glanced over at Vera. Her head was back, her eyes were closed, and her hands were in her lap. Two of her fingers were twitching. I doubted if Vera could go back now. The introverted wallflower was gone for good and I, for one, was damned glad to see her gone. Free spirit Vera was a far happier person.

***

We got checked into a two-bedroom suite, went potty, and changed into comfortable evening attire.

Darcy made a phone call from the bar in our sitting room then we went downstairs for an early dinner.

Nothing was mentioned at the table concerning our impending foray into the "darker side" of sexual awareness, but saying I was anxious about what was to come of it would be putting it mildly. And, my anxiety was growing by leaps and bounds as I haphazardly toyed with my food.

Barb seemed anxious, too, but I knew it was because she was well aware of what would be coming our way.

Vera was quiet, almost subdued, but her eyes hadn't lost one miniscule of the intense sparkle they had developed on the way to where we were sitting now.

Just about the time we were ready to get up, Darcy's cell phone went off in her purse. Her eyes went wide with surprise. She recovered her composure and said, "Fine," into her cell phone. "Just you and Willie, huh? Should still be enough to get the job done." She swept her eyes around the table. "If we're not there in ten minutes, then we won't be there at all." She flipped the cell phone closed. "Your after-dinner chocolate mints are waiting upstairs, ladies." Her tone hardened, leaving none of us any wiggle room. "Any of you who do not wish to partake, better see if the hotel has another room available."

"Not on a bet," Barb said. "I didn't come this far to wind up sleeping all alone."

"Count me in," Vera said with noticeable excitement in her voice.

They all three looked at me. "Well?" Darcy insisted. "This whole thing was supposed to be for your ah... your education."

Nothing here was hinging on my decision. I could get another room and let Barb and Vera go ahead with this. But, I wasn't about to. Like Barb, I hadn't come this far to sleep alone, and like Vera, I had to find out for myself. If I chickened out, I would forever wonder what it was like.

I stood up and grabbed my purse. "Let's go see what our after-dinner chocolate mints look like."

"And how good they feel," Barb added, snagging her own purse from under her chair.

Vera grinned as she shoved her chair back and nearly leapt to her feet. "And just how good they have got to taste, don't forget."

Back upstairs, Darcy ran the magnetic card through the slot and entered first, then moved to the side and introduced us as we filed in. "This is Liz, and Barb, and Vera. Ladies, this is Reese, and that good for nothin' black cowpoke leaning against the bar is Willie G."

My eyes washed over the man she had introduced as Reese. He was a good looking man, six foot six (or thereabouts) with a lean athletic build and the wavy hairstyle Nat King Cole had favored. His coloring was that of milk chocolate, soft and creamy, a couple of shades darker than a good tan and he sported a clean, military-trimmed mustache under his chiseled nose. Attired in a pair of dark chocolate slacks and a pale yellow polo shirt, with what looked like tasseled Gucci loafers on his feet, a gold chain ID bracelet on one wrist, casually holding a Perrier in his other hand, he could have just stepped off the cover of GQ. I felt myself melt from the inside out. Meaning that my still moist panties became just a bit moister.

I forcibly pulled my gaze from this handsome hunk of chocolate heaven to appraise at the other man in the room. Five foot seven, maybe five-eight and sinewy, dressed in tight, well-worn jeans, a white western snap-front shirt open at the throat, shiny black cowboy boots, a black Stetson tilled back on his head, and a cold Coors clutched in his hand, a black cowpoke had certainly been an accurate description of Willie G. His welcoming, "Evening, ladies," spoken in a deep Negro voice with a western twang would have been comical if it hadn't gone so perfectly with his cowboy outfit and his dark chocolate complexion.

Reese walked over to us. (He almost seemed to glide across the floor to me.) "Since slow poke over there probably won't think of it," he said in an educated voice (Literally dripping with sensuality.) "can I offer you ladies something to drink?"

Up close, I could see that Reese's almond eyes were almost violet. "Co...Coke," I stammered. "A Coke will be just fine." I didn't want my mind clouded in the least by hard liquor for the rest of the night.

"I want something stronger," I heard Barb say. "Tequila. Quervo Gold if you've got it."

"I want a beer," Vera chirped.

"Comin' right up, little lady," Willie G drawled. Reaching into the small fridge under the bar, he pulled out another Coors, popped the tab as he crossed the floor and handed it to Vera. He jauntily tapped his can against hers. "Bottoms up, Vera."

As long as I've known her, I had never seen Vera touch a beer, let alone drink one. But, with her eyes fixed on Willie G's, she bottomed up her can and drained it right along with him like she had been chug-a-lugging all her life. She was coughing and sputtering by the time her can was empty, but she grinned and handed Willie the can. "Now, how about one I can taste, Cowboy."

"Gal after my own heart," Willie laughed.

That loosened everything up considerably. Some soft background music (Which cowpoke Willie sneered at.) was put on and in no time a cocktail party of mixed personalities, sexes, and races might as well have been taking place in our suite. Reese ("When he wasn't occupied being one damned hot chocolate mint."), it turned out, was a private investigator for several of the casinos and amateur writer. And I was quickly of the opinion that this suave sleuth ("And try saying the 3 times fast... without fucking it up, especially with your mouth watering.") Anyway, this enticing mocha gumshoe could investigate me ("All of me!") all he wanted, and for as long as he wished, just as long as he didn't write about it afterward.

"That would be the same as kissing and telling," Reese informed me with a beguiling grin when I made this wish known to him. "And a gentleman never does that. Not a true gentleman." God, even his seductive voice was making me wet by now.

Willie G was exactly what his dress and boots and hat, his western twang, and his layback attitude proclaimed him to be; a cowboy. A PRCA sanctioned bull rider, he worked on one of the outlying ranches during the off season. (That's Professional Rodeo Cowboy Association for those of you not in the know.)

Barb sort of bounced back and forth between the two guys, spending some time chatting amicably with Reese or over by the bar joking a bit cruder with Willie G. Vera exchanged pleasantries with Reese, always with a warm smile, but I noticed she never strayed very far from Willie. Even apart from him her eyes were almost constantly on Willie G Former wallflower Vera was acting like a smitten schoolgirl.

There was definitely something between Darcy and Reese. She was cordial, even openly friendly. She would laugh when he made a joke. (Only a few of which could be considered off-color.) She would listen attentively when something more serious was being discussed. But, she was clearly keeping her distance from him. She had told us ahead of time that she would not be an active participant in this, so I figured that was what had to be behind the line of demarcation she was steadfastly maintaining.

It was a pleasant, relaxed atmosphere and I almost forgot the reason behind our pleasant cocktail party. Until Barb changed the entire tone of the evening by thumping her empty shot glass down on the bar and asking in a too loud voice, "Well, is something hot and wet and sexy going to happen here tonight, or not?"

A pregnant hush fell over the room and Barb's, Vera's, and Darcy's eyes turned to me. Then I felt Reese's smoldering eyes on me and finally Willie G's.

Talk about feeling like a deer trapped in the headlights of an oncoming semi. That was yours truly... goose bumps and all.

Part 5

I was incredibly horny and that was underestimating the present state of my libido. That I was beyond anxious for this, or at least something, to happen would have been putting it mildly. That it was time to shit, or get the hell off the quandary pot was without question.

'Do it!' I firmly told myself and got up off the couch. I marched across the room to the wet bar, spotted a bottle of Chevis Regal, poured three fingers into a glass and drank it down it two swallows. A minor tremor shook me as the raw liquor burnt its way down to my flip-flopping belly. Sufficiently buoyed with liquid courage, I set the glass back on the bar, turned around, and leaned back against it.

"All right," I said bravely, "let's get this show on the road." I had my choice of two men, but I fixed my eyes squarely on the man I'd, hours earlier, decided I wanted most. "Reese," I said in as strong a voice as I could manage, "why don't you show me, and all the rest of us, what you've got to offer."

Reese smiled at my boldness and he smoothly hoisted his loose-fitting polo shirt over his head. He folded the shirt and laid it over the arm of the couch then lifted his feet one at a time to remove his Gucci loafers and dark brown socks. He put the folded socks inside the shoes then unbuckled his belt. The hiss of his lowered zipper was the only sound in the anxious room. His slacks were carefully folded and laid on top of his shirt, leaving Reese clad in only a pair of abbreviated cream-colored boxer shorts. He met my anxious gaze evenly, then skinned his shorts off and laid them atop the rest of his clothing. I was now facing, in person, at my first naked black man and I looked him up and very appraisingly. A gold nugget the size of my thumbnail hung from a gold chain around his neck and there was some curly black hair on his solid chest, but it was sparse. His stomach was flat, his hips were narrow, and his leg muscles were well defined. I'd been right in my initial assessment of the man; Reese was definitely a man who took care of himself... very good care, indeed. My appraising gaze centered itself just below his trim midsection. At this point, it was his cock I was most interested in. Hanging down beneath a mat of black, crinkly hair, it was darker (as most cocks generally are) then the rest of his sculptured milk chocolate body and was uncircumcised. Other than being surprisingly still flaccid, it looked pretty normal in size. 'Possibly a bit thicker than normal', I thought to myself and couldn't wait to see how impressive it might become when he found something inspiring enough to get it up.

"Okay," Reese challenged, "your turn, Liz."

"You want this prize," I brazenly challenged right back, "you're gonna have to come over here and unwrap it yourself." With an understanding nod, he came over to me. My eyes never left his mesmerizing chocolate cock, swaying heavily back and forth like an imposing black pendulum as he crossed the silent room. Even when he had come to a stop less than a foot in front of me, my eyes remained riveted on the ebony object of my present dark obsession.

"Here's one of those opportunities to say stop, Liz." I said nothing. I couldn't trust myself to speak. I raised my eyes and met his without blinking. Our eyes now locked with each other's, he unbuttoned my blouse. He slid it off my shoulders and down my arms and off my shaking hands, then folded it neatly and placed it on the bar. He undid the button on my skirt, unzipped it then lowered it to the floor so I could step out of it and then folded it, too. I kicked off my own sandals. Reese leaned in to reach behind me and undo my bra. I broke my gaze with his searching eyes and looked down. I could still see the floor between us. We weren't touching, yet it felt like his naked body was being pressed against my own. He properly folded the bra (cup folded inside opposing cup) and set it on the bar, then with his hands on my hips, he went down on his knees. His fingers curled inside the waistband of my panties, he looked up.

"Another one of those opportunities, Liz?" I didn't say anything again. I didn't need to. Reese knew I wasn't going to stop him. I could feel and, from his much closer vantage point, he could see that the crotch of my panties was sodden with my flowing juices, rendering it, essentially, a useless strip of nearly see-through cloth. He peeled my panties down my legs, allowed me to step out of them, then set them off to the side before standing back up.

"What do you want, Liz?" Now that, gentlemen, is what is known as sexual courtesy. Not how did I want it, but what did I want.

"Everything," I answered. I hadn't come this far to settle for a simple slam-bam-thank-you-ma'am quickie. "I want it all, Reese. All I can get." Reese's cock was at last coming to life. "And I do mean of all you've got." With a nod of understanding, Reese wrapped his hands around my waist and lifted me onto the bar. My breath caught in my throat when my hot ass made contact with the cold marble. He gently pressed my knees apart and leaned in. With his mouth poised at my pussy, he raised his eyes to mine.

"One more opportunity, Liz?" "Do ittttt!" I hissed, and I damned near crawled out of my skin when he kissed me in the most intimate of ways. I had heard somewhere, from someone (I don't remember who, or when, or how many times) that black men didn't eat pussy, that they didn't like it. Well, I'm here to tell you that, whoever the ill-informed dolt was, they didn't know what the hell they were talking about. Reese not only knew how to eat pussy; he clearly enjoyed his oral labors. He knew just how to kiss my outer lips, how to gently spread them apart and kiss inside. He knew just how to work my clit with his tongue and lips and how to slowly lick the length of my slit. And, when I leaned back on my hands to give him more access to my yearning cunt, he knew just how to work that amazingly long and fantastic tongue into my steamy hole. Reese ate me out as well, if not better, then (to that point in time, anyway) I've ever been eaten out in my entire life, giving me two shuddering orgasms in the process. But Reese didn't stop pleasuring me. I had demanded everything, and he was going to see to that I got just what I asked for... and in black on white spades. ("Pun intended.") He continued to superbly eat my pussy, tonguing my unhooded and aching clit and sucking it between his lips before sliding down and deeply tongue-fucking my slippery cunthole.

He made me cum a third time, this time with my feet up on his shoulders and my quivering ass way up off the bar. When I at last caught my breath, I decided it would only be polite to return such an absolutely wonderful favor. Pushing Reese back from the bar, I slid off and continued on down until I was kneeling before him. His black cock was now rock hard and staring me right in the face. I wrapped my hand around it, excited as much by the stark contrast of white on black as by what I was about to do; suck off a hard, black cock. Reese's cock was hot to the touch and felt thicker than Brad's. It also appeared to be longer. Well, I had always heard that black men had impressive cocks, hadn't I? I stroked my fist up its turgid black length. A drop of clear precum oozed from the pisshole. I swiped it away with the flat of my tongue then kissed the dark purple head of his cock. I teased at the piss hole with the tip of my tongue then closed my lips over the head. I found the taste of black cock different than white cock. Not a bad difference, just different.

Excitingly different. I now had the swollen head of my first black dick in my mouth.

How much of it could I take? 'Only one way to find that out'. I slid my mouth down on it, taking in two inches. I pulled back then slid back down onto four inches of it. The head of Reese's cock was now at the opening to my throat, and I hadn't gagged yet. 'Oh, just go for it', I told myself as I pulled my mouth back. And, with one impetuous forward lunge of my head, I took the entire thing into my mouth and down my throat. With my lips pressed into his crinkly black pubic hair, I was a trifle surprised that I had deep-throated him so easily, until I realized that Reese wasn't any more well-endowed than Brad. He was thicker, true, but where his hard, plump cockhead was now lodged in my throat felt to be about half an inch short of where Brad's cockhead normally reached.

Reese's cock had only appeared to be more impressive because it had been black. 'So', I wondered as I began giving that forbidden black cock some serious head, 'just how much of this black-cocks-are-bigger-than-white-cocks thing was physical, and how much of it was purely psychological'? As if that insignificant difference made any difference in the present scheme of things. I had that cock easily fucking my throat and now had only one goal in mind; making Reese's black cock shoot off and give me a taste of my first load of black man's cum. I cupped his balls in the palm of my hand. They were big and heavy, full of cum. Hot, delicious cum that I wanted, and wanted damned quick. I pulled my mouth off Reese's cock and raised my eyes.

"Don't even bother making with another of those 'opportunity' things this time," I told him and went right back down on him. Massaging his cum-bloated balls, it only took another dozen mouth-fucks for him to be close. The cockhead imbedded in my throat swelled noticeably, then Reese's bloated balls sucked up tight in his scrotum, meaning he was right there. I quickly took that black cock all the way to the root and swallowed hard. Instantly, a hot jet of cum blasted down my throat, then another... and then another. I pulled back and held the head tightly behind my lips as his throbbing cock ejaculated twice more into my mouth. I continued to suck on the swollen head, and also a couple of inches of that nice thick cock, coaxing every last dribble and ooze of cum from his balls. I held the salty/sweet, slimy mixture in my mouth, swirling it around and around the head of his cock, savoring the rich, creamy taste of his cum before pulling my mouth off his cock. I then leaned my head back, with my mouth wide open so he could see all that slimy, milky-white cum in my mouth and slowly, very slowly, swallowed every last yummy rivulet of it. Orgasmic shivers ran through me as that cum slid down my throat. I waited until it had all (And I do mean all of it) hit bottom before smiling up at Reese.

"Well?" "Liz, you have got one wicked mouth." He reached down and tenderly laid his hand against my cheek.

"And one mean-ass throat." I winked at him.

"So I've been told." I kissed and laved the head of his cock with the flat of my tongue before taking it back in my mouth and thoroughly cleaning it of all my spit and his cum. And that I happily swallowed, too. I was so ready to get fucked by now that I would have taken on a breeding stallion. I held on to Reese's still-fairly-erect cock as I sat down and rolled onto my back.

"Please tell me you've got at least one more of those huge, healthy loads left in you."

"We'll just have to see," he answered as he knelt between my spread and elevated knees. "Won't we?"

"We damned well better do more than just see," I growled as I literally pulled his thick, quickly stiffening, black cock into the opening of my hot, soupy cunt. I was so fucking wet it went all the way in with just one thrust of Reese's hips. All the way to his balls slapping against my wet asscheeks.

"Now, let's fuck!" I love cock. I love having a cock in my cunt almost as much as I love having one down my throat. Plain and simple, I love to fuck. I love Brad fucking me. And, I was really, really, enjoying having this good-looking black man fucking his big, black cock into me. And I was enjoying the hell out of fucking him right back. Reese thrust his great black cock into me time after glorious time and I hunched my hot cunt onto his black cock with just as much fucking enthusiasm. I came, then immediately came again. Reese hooked his arms behind my knees and lifted so that my feet were draped over his shoulders, elevating my cunt so he could really pound it to me. I rose up on my elbows so I could watch his glistening black cock fucking in and out of my brunette-haired, pink-inside-white cunt. I was exciting, exhilarating beyond belief.

"Liz, I going to..."

"Don't you dare pull out!" I nearly screamed. "I want to feel your hot jizz shooting into me."

"But...?"

"I'm on the pill," I anxiously told him. "You just keep fucking me like you're, Baby, and..." My cunt muscles clamped down around his pistoning cock in a quick, hard orgasm. "Ohhhhhhhhh, for the love of Goddd!!!" The unexpected climax subsided just as fast as it had hit.

"And," I continued when I got draw a breath, "when you're ready to blow, I want you to bury every single inch of that wonderful black cock of yours into this horny white lady's hot, juicy cunt and shoot your hot jizz all the way up into my mouth."

I blew him a puckered wet kiss. "I really do like the taste of your cum, Baby." The cords in Reese's neck were standing out.

"I don't know if I can shoot far... far enough for you to... to taste, but... here... it... it... CUMMMMMMSSSSSsssssssss!!!!!!!" "ffffffffffff... FFFFFFUUUUUCCCCCKKKKKKK!!!!!" I screamed as the first hard blast of Reese's hot jizz shot into me.

Then my cunt received a second blast of hot jizz, and a third, and a forth. I came with the second blast, and the third, and the forth. Reese quickly pulled out of my convulsing cunt and just about the time I started to come down from my orgasmic high, he plunged that wondrous hard, black cock of his all the way back into me. And that, readers, is when the bright lights went out in Vegas for one extremely well fucked white lady.

Magdelina
Part 1

The city awoke with the morning sunrise that day. The village was dancing and the maidens were happy for news had come. Their men were coming home from the crusades which they set out for almost 2 years previous. The men had left promising to conquer the holy land. Yet what really happened was even further from the truth.

***

Allan of Gale had left the kingdom to make his own legend. He also left behind his maiden in waiting, his father, and the rest of his family. He left it all for his ego ran higher than all the hills in the county. Allan had yearned for the spotlight and although he knew he was in line to be the next king, he wanted to make his own name. He was betrothed to Lady Magdelina, the king's daughter. Their father's had arranged for the marriage, and Allan then knew he was set.

Knowing he was to be wed to the King's daughter, Allan set out with his other friends, to be heroes in the crusades. When word spread the holy land was not being won Allan rethought his plan. The crusades failed since so many "noble" knights set out and wasted their time, pillaging the land in every way. Allan was no different. However, he went in a different direction.

Allan strayed from the normal route and led himself and his friends, venturing far from the holy land and pillaged small towns further east. They took whatever they could and sent letters back to their homeland, decrying their valor and how they fought to vanquish the holy land of their now evil inhabitants.

***

Lady Magdelina, known as "Maggie" to her friends, had a bounce to her step as she walked up the numerous stairs in the castle tower. She had just read a letter from her Allan. He wrote her promising he would be returning home with many gifts. "Oh what a grand hero's welcome he'll receive" she thought to herself.

Maggie loved to walk the steps in the castle. As a young girl she would run up those stairs to escape her caretakers who couldn't match her athleticism or youthful exuberance. She would run up the steps which led to the top room of a tower in the castle. That room was her special place where she would go and talk with her aide Eleanor. She was the one woman Maggie could confide in and trust.

She got to her room and stood in front of the mirror which her father had bought for her. It was one of her favorite things. Mirrored glass was so rare and expensive it was perhaps her most enjoyed possession. She took a brush and began to comb her long blonde hair. She proceeded to take off the large skirt that was making her too hot on this humid, summer day.

Lady Magdelina had always been the most beautiful woman in the land. Her long blonde hair framed her angelic flawless face. She began to untie her corset which she really had no need for. While

208

most women wore them to keep their bellies in, her stomach was tight, and taught. It was slender and thin, although she had to wear the corset too support her rather large breasts. They stood large and proud, she didn't even need the corset for them as they could stand beautifully on their own. She wore it though to cover her rather large nipples which would protrude through any kind of slim material.

Maggie also removed the stockings from her legs, they were muscular and well formed. The years of riding horses and running up the steps gave her calves and legs a shape that would put anyone to shame. The running up the steps also helped to contribute the buttocks which stood so proudly from her backside. When she stood straight up naked her breasts and buttocks stood out from her body, and both were full and round.

She didn't look at herself naked in the mirror except when she would take her scissors and carefully trim her pubic hair. The hot summer days made it necessary for her to keep her hair to a short covering so as not to cause that much irritation as she got sweaty running up her beloved stairs.

Now Allan and herself could climb the stairs together and share their lives together. "Oh my brave warrior is coming home. I can only count the days till he arrives." she thought to herself.

***

The town's people cheered as the young men returned to a jubilant ovation. Unlike so many young men who had set out for the crusades all the young men of that city made it back home. Then again these so-called crusaders hadn't exactly been fighting as much as they had told the town.

The men came back riding unusually large horses and also drawing carriages carrying all kinds of spices, silk and a man walking behind them with a sack on his face with only eyeholes cut out so he could see where he walked. The people saw that the man's hands were black and immediately people began to talk. For a moor had made his way to the town.

A celebration went on throughout that night. Torches and fires lit the Darkness and music filled everyone with joy. Dancing and drinking consumed the night away and Allan and Maggie had gotten back together. They talked through the night.

"Oh Maggie I've missed you incredibly. It is so good to be back home."

"Allan how I've waited for you. You must tell me of your adventures. It's a miracle you came back. I had heard stories of men being murdered and killed in the holy land, I prayed every day for your safe return."

"There will be plenty of time to discuss my adventures later. However, I did promise you a present. Come with me."

Allan took Maggie's hand as he led her to one of the carriages filled with goods. He showed her the tons of gold and silks he had brought back. "Oh Allan this is all so beautiful. But I only care that you are here now and safe." She turned around to see Allan guiding the hooded man towards her.

"Yes but I've brought you, well actually he's more of my gift to myself, a slave. I bought him through a trader in a town on the outskirts of the holy land." With that Allan took the hood off and showed off the slave he had bought. Maggie had never in her life seen a colored man although he had a ruggedly handsome face. "Allan! How can you buy a man to be your slave? You cannot buy a person." Maggie told him.

Allan answered back a bit abruptly. "Maggie, he's one of the few negroes that can also speak English. He used to be a prince in his land, and how is he different than your servants and the indentured servants that work for your father. Go ahead say hello, Tepus."

"Hello madam." Tepus answered in a deep rich voice. His strong stare met her gentle blue eyes. Tepus had never seen a woman of such beauty. She had large breasts like the women in his tribe. She possessed a posterior like those women as well, yet she was slender everywhere else. Allan noticed him staring at Maggie's generous cleavage. Allan kicked him in the leg, "Keep your eyes to yourself, slave!"

Allan then led the slave and tied him to the back of the carriage. He proceeded to accompany Maggie away, back to the party. "Allan?" Maggie asked in a soft voice.

"Yes dearest." Allan answered.

"Promise me you'll treat him like a person. He is a person, don't treat him as some animal. Treat him like an apprentice. Even my lowest servants live in the castle and have comfortable lives. Promise me please." She begged him.

Allan said nothing. Maggie saw how indecisive he was. He obviously didn't share her view on the subject.

"Please" she said to reaffirm her position.

Allan stared down at her supple bosom and felt a stirring in his pants.

"I promise, love. On one condition..." Allan told her.

"Yes Allan?" she answered quizzically.

"Satisfy me here in this carriage. Quickly no one will see and it's been long since I have touched you." Allan explained to her even though he had regularly raped women on his "crusade". Before he left they had consummated and Maggie felt nothing, however after so long she too felt a stirring in her loins that perhaps now could be satisfied.

Allan opened a door to one of the carriages he brought filled with silken linens. They laid on top as Allan kissed and fondled Maggie. He quickly lifted her long skirt and unfastened himself. He quickly entered his rigid, itching manhood into her waiting pussy. He thrust himself strongly and quickly into Maggie. He held her by her slim waist and furiously pounded himself into her. After several more thrusts he left his seed in her and fell back.

Maggie looked up, disappointed to see him tucking in his now shriveling penis. It wasn't as large as she had remembered it. It didn't last as long either. She quickly made herself back up and they made their way back to the celebration.

***

That night the two lovers stole away from the party back to the castle. They were in the stairwell that led to Maggie's room. They kissed and grabbed at each other savagely.

Maggie moaned as he kissed her neck, "Oh Allan carry me to my room, make love to me once more."

Allan had spent many a night with whores while he was away. He had violated many other women too and knew that he could only perform once per night. For some reason, he had difficulty reviving after such a rush of passion. He planned to carry her to her room and then use that as an excuse to explain why he was spent.

He took her in his arms, "To the top love?" he asked her. She shook her head yes staring into his eyes. Their lips met again. They never made it to the top.

Allan tired quickly and set her down on the spiral staircase. Maggie was feeling quite rambunctious and said, "Allan...if you don't beat me to my room then you'll never know my pleasures again tonight." She quickly ran up the stairs as she had for so many years. Her muscular legs sending her upwards. Allan just laid there on the steps. Feeling the effects of the wine he had consumed that night.

"All the better. There would have been nothing for me to do up there." he thought to himself as he fell asleep on the stairs.

***

213

2 months had passed. Maggie was in her room topless as her aide Eleanor sewed a new corset, trying to fit it to her. Eleanor was a lovely maiden with brown hair which she always wore in a bun. Like Maggie, she was thin and athletic, though her breasts were nowhere near the size of Magdelina's. As she held pins in her teeth the two chatted.

"You know Maggie the word is all around town." Eleanor said.

"Do you think it's true? Allan would never do such a thing." Magdelina asked honestly, her breasts shaking as she looked behind her turning to see Eleanor sewing.

"They say Allan sired the child over 2 years ago. It could have been before he left for the crusades. The boy is three now and has his eyes."

"I could not believe that. Besides Eleanor, Allan has made love to me and he barely has the stamina nor physical prowess to sire a child."

Both women giggled. "Perhaps later we can go to the brook. I could use the long walk, besides the heat is sweltering today.

***

Both women wore gowns that were easy to get out of as they made their way through town. They had to walk, out to the middle of the forest where there was a warm water spring. Even in winter the spring would steam. Rumors had said a dragon's lair stayed underneath warming the ground below the lake and warming it. The townspeople had been forbidden from the brook by the King, the king's daughter however, loved the brook and swam in it regularly. Since it was enclosed privacy came easily. No one could see or stumble upon it in the dense forest unless they knew the correct location.

As they made their way through the town, Eleanor pointed to a young boy and whispered to Maggie, "Look that is the child, there is the mother."

"Eleanor, I recognize the town whore. However, the child looks new to me. He is a young, handsome one though."

As they spoke the child ran to its mother. The town whore, whose name was Anne. She had a generous bust like Maggie, and tanned skin with black curly hair. She lifted the child in her arms and walked into her living quarters. As she walked back the child looked at Maggie holding its thumb. It was then that Maggie saw the child's eyes. They were exactly like Allan's.

"Could it be true Eleanor? If it was do they see one another, now that he has returned?" Maggie asked her aide.

It was at that moment that Eleanor's mother had found her just as they were about to leave the gates of the castle grounds. "Sorry Maggie I must attend to something, I'll be at the brook shortly go on without me."

***

Maggie made her way to the brook with ease. Since her childhood, she had made her way to this brook where the trees broke just enough to illuminate all of its water surface with rich sunlight.

Maggie took a look around and lifted her dress over her head. In her underwear, she began to untie her corset when she heard the water moving. She took a deep breath and bent down in the tall grass to see what it could be. She looked through the grass to see a man emerging from the water. It was Allan's slave. It was unmistakable since he was the only black man perhaps within a thousand miles. She watched as the water cascaded down his body. Years of hard work had forged his body into rippling muscles. He had some scars on his back and she watched in awe as his muscles flexed while he shook the water from himself. Then she saw something incredible.

When Maggie had taken Allan to this brook before he left on his journey, they swam naked. The water had shrunk Allan to the size of a grape. She laughed but this time another naked man was here and she could only rub her eyes to see that they weren't playing tricks with her. From Tepus' crotch hung the thickest, black penis imaginable. It hung from his pubic hair almost to his knee. Maggie had seen something bobbing before when she had met him and he wore his baggy rags but this was a monstrosity.

She gasped loudly, causing Tepus to quickly look around. Maggie brought her hand to her mouth. Tepus quickly saw the blonde hair in the tall grass and walked to her, not bothering to cover himself. They made eye contact, until Maggie's eyes returned to this monstrous penis.

"Are you lost?" He asked her in that deep masculine voice.

"I think you are the one that is lost, this is my brook." Maggie said standing up. Maggie forgot she was in her underwear and corset. Her corset only covered and supported the bottom half of her breasts and her nipples and aureoles were in view.

"This is my bathing area. Sorry but I have never seen you here. You are the princess correct?"

"Yes I am, sorry but I have never seen anyone here before. I too come here to bathe. I am sorry for my outburst. It is open to all, even though the king said it's forbidden from townspeople. Then again I don't think that applies to you." Maggie said that without any malice and true honesty.

"I suppose." Tepus said sadly.

"Is Allan treating you well? I asked him to give you decent housing and food? Are you being well taken care off?" Maggie asked. Her eyes occasionally sneaking peaks at the large penis dangling back and forth as Tepus swayed.

"I suppose, Allan has given me sleeping quarters in his barn and the meals are ok." Tepus answered noticing Maggie's heavier breathing, and her nipples hardening.

"That is wonderful, if you don't mind me asking, how did a moor like you, who can speak such English wind up in the holy land?"

Tepus looked at her quizzically, "I used to be royalty in my land like you. I was a prince but my arrogance and temper cost me. I killed a man and my father said to earn my place as royalty I had to become a slave for 5 moon cycles. Then I must make my way back to become king."

Maggie took all this in, did savages really have kings and queens? It seemed odd but not entirely impossible. "I understand your predicament, do you know how much longer you must be indentured?"

Tepus answered, "I watch the moon every day, I will know when I must make my way back. Until then I must serve whoever owns me. Your husband, bought me in a land far east. I am not sure if this is the holy land you speak of."

A rustling came in the bushes now, Maggie quickly realized the situation she was in. She looked down once again at how Tepus' penis jiggled as he too looked around.

Looking down also made Maggie notice her nipples and breasts were in full view. Sweat making them glisten in the sun. "Quickly you must go! should someone see us they surely would kill you." Maggie said touching his shoulder urging him on. She felt a jolt of warmth and electricity at the touch of his dark skin. He quickly gathered his rags and made his way into the trees.

Eleanor came through the trees moments later. "Sorry Maggie, hope I didn't startle you. You haven't even undressed fully. How nice of you to wait. "

Tepus put his rags on and watched the two women undress and begin to play in the water. Respecting their privacy and before his cock could harden more he made his way back to his stable. To sleep next to his neighbor the horse.

***

The next day there was a great joust, and tourney taking place. In the royal stands Maggie sat next to her betrothed, Sir Allan. Tepus was there standing next to Allan. Throughout the day he had to taste Allan's food to see if it was poisoned. He also fetched everything the royal's wanted. Maggie stole glances at his crotch and thought to herself, "It would be a shame if he was poisoned. To waste a man with such a gift...."

Maggie's thinking was interrupted when she saw Allan was making eye contact with someone in the crowd. There was Anne, the town whore. Allan whispered Tepus a message and sent him out into the crowd. Maggie said nothing and watched, she saw Tepus make his way behind Anne and say something, behind her ear. Maggie excused herself and made her way behind the royal stands.

As Tepus approached Maggie said in a stern voice, "What did you say to that woman!"

Tepus was now frightened that perhaps she would kill him for talking to a white woman. How the whites changed when they saw him alone and when they saw him fraternizing with their kind.

"I wasn't saying anything to her. I have no interest in her, I don't mean to do anything to her..." Tepus said in a very apologetic tone.

"I know you're not one to fuck the town whore! So what did Allan tell you to tell her? Is he making love to her?" Maggie asked sternly checking to see if anyone was eavesdropping.

Tepus was in a bad situation, he thought to himself whether he should betray his lord or lie to her. If she didn't get what she wanted she might scream he tried to touch her and he would be a dead man for sure. Out of fear he surrendered the information.

"He meets her often in his house next to the stable. half past sundown they meet in his house. I know not what they do but they meet again tonight." Tepus told her.

Her angelic face had become one of worry. "Thank you Tepus, I forever owe you for your honesty. Go quickly before they think something is amiss." with that Tepus made his way back as Maggie made plans.

Maggie waited a bit, and then returned to her seat. The jousting was picking up and nearing the end. The crowd cheered loudly and as she went to sit down her chair broke a leg and sent her crashing to the ground on her well-shaped ass. Some laughed but most rushed to her aid. Since the royal seats were higher then where the peasants and townspeople stood very few really saw what had happened.

"Oh drat I ruined my chair how will I watch the jousting. Your friend Mark will soon be here to fight won't he, Allan?" Maggie asked a bit breathlessly. Allan had an evil grin as he thought of a fantastic solution. he knew of his slave's lust for his maiden. He saw the way Tepus would look at his princess. He wanted to tease his enslaved black.

Allan said to Maggie, "Dear just sit on the table. You will be able to watch the jousting even better."

"Splendid Idea Allan." Maggie said, she had no problem sitting on the table since the food had long since been eaten.

"Ah Ah Ah" Allan said, "You still need some cushion, and your fair body should not sit upon this filthy retched dirty table. Here, Slave NOW! You will be her seat lay on the table."

Maggie was frightened by this. Was Allan mad? Use a human being as a seat? "SLAVE!!! Lay on the table and let my woman use you as a chair." Allan said kicking Tepus. Tepus laid on the table and Maggie took a seat on his knees. Allan ordered Tepus to lay his head and back on the table so he could not watch the jousting.

Maggie looked at Allan strangely. This was not the man she had remembered who had left two years ago. She sat upon Tepus' knees and his thick thighs. Just then she felt her buttocks touch what was the head of Tepus' penis. "Oh goodness" she thought. Her vagina began to warm itself. The closeness of their body was causing Tepus to grow. His dick began to lengthen and poke Maggie in her buttocks.

"Goodness should he keep hardening surely his rags will raise and they will kill him for his arousal." Maggie thought as she quickly, so as not to arouse suspicion, put her hands on the table and raised herself. She came down with her ass on more of his penis to keep if flat against his legs. It would be safe till the end of the match.

His fattening penis felt so strong and thick. It felt as if it fit between her ass cheeks perfectly filling her crack.

The jousting finally ended and Maggie rose off Tepus who quickly sat up and walked away hunched over to hide his semi-aroused state. Maggie then walked to the castle. She would get her payback tonight.

***

She planned on catching Allan tonight. She would hide in the top of his stable which had no wall underneath the roofing. Where the hay would stick out she could easily see the part of his home which had the most windows. She would wait till they finished their session, run down and catch them. She made her way into the stable luckily the door was open. Her muscular thighs flexed as she went up the ladder and took her place in the hay. She had taken a telescopic looking glass Allan had brought back with him. He said a magician had made it.

She would use it to catch him, his gift would be his undoing. Maggie nestled in the hay and fell asleep, she would awake at nightfall hopefully.

***

Maggie opened her eyes to see stars. It was dark for sure, She got out her looking glass and looked for light in Allan's house. She saw a candle in a window on the first floor. She looked through the looking glass and then saw an arm. A woman's

222

arm. She watched in horror as Allan, who was naked, laid down the town whore Anne and carefully entered her with his penis. Her black curly pubic hair meeting his as they ground into each other sweatily.

Thanks to Allan's great loving Maggie didn't have to wait long. Allan soon finished and collapsed naked next to the whore on the floor. Maggie knew this was her chance. As she turned around to get to the ladder she heard a woman scream. "Aaaaaaahhhhhh AAAhhhhhhhh!" The scream sounded as if someone was shaking the woman. It sounded like Eleanor! To hell with Allan's infidelity she would have more opportunities to catch him. Her dearest friend was in trouble and she sounded nearby.

Eleanor's voice came again. "OOoooohhhhh mmmyyyyy......Teeeepppppuuusss!"

"TEPUS?!" Maggie thought, they sounded as though they were below her. Just then she remembered that the stable was Tepus' home. Maggie crawled slowly to the opening where the ladder was. She held her long blonde hair behind her as she peered down.

There was Eleanor, her dress lifted up above her waist and top pulled down, bunched up around her waist. Eleanor was on all fours as she saw Tepus pounding into her friend from behind. "OOOOOHHHHHHHHH YYYESSSSSSS!!!" Eleanor growled through gritted teeth. Maggie had never seen Eleanor like this. The lovely girl was rutting like some wild animal.

Tepus ran his long fingers along her sides and reached under her to fondle her small breasts and little brown nipples. Sweat dripped from their bodies. Maggie looked at her lifelong friend in awe. She had never seen her like this. Long strands of her hair had come from her bun and clung to the sides of her face as she made odd faces, both of them grunting like maniacs. Her slender back led down to her trim ass, and Tepus muscular midsection pounded against it making slapping sounds.

"How could any man enter a woman from behind in such position." Maggie thought, soon realizing the silliness of her question as she remembered the size of Tepus' member. More than once Eleanor would put her face to the ground and lay there motionless as Tepus held her slim ass tightly as he pounded her moistness.

Tepus began to moan louder and pump faster, when Eleanor put her hand to him to slow him, "I cannot sire a child, please withdraw yourself, there would be no mistaking whooooooo ooooo o" Eleanor stopped herself as he furiously gave himself to her. Grabbing her bun of hair. He then withdrew completely, Maggie's eyes widened. What she had saw at the brook was nothing compared to this.

His cock when aroused was so much bigger, bigger than she ever imagined. Her concentration was broken as Eleanor's face attached itself to the head of the large swollen monster. She greedily sucked on him and moved her tiny hand along its vast, thick shaft. He then screamed a primal scream and his semen came flowing shooting all over

Eleanor's face. To Maggie's horror she saw Eleanor trying to drink the white substance. Maggie was also amazed at the amount that had been spewed forth by the black snake.

Eleanor then wiped herself with her gown, she kissed Tepus deeply, Maggie watched as their tongues intertwined. After a long moment, the very satisfied brunette put her gown back on and said, "I have to go before suspicions are aroused, perhaps another time."

Eleanor made her way out of the barn as Tepus just sat with his arms back on a stack of hay. His penis still standing a foot in the air. Coated in the juices of two human beings who had enjoyed each other's company immensely.

It then struck Maggie how was she to get out of this mess. The guards might soon start looking for her. She thought of waiting till Tepus went to sleep but then those hopes were dashed as the barn door moved.

Anne walked into the barn door, just holding her gown on her arm in front of her she dropped it exposing her naked body to Tepus. Maggie liked the look of Anne's body. She exuded sexuality. The two were an extremely erotic scene. her long curly black hair hung to her waist, her left breast covered by the hair hanging. her ass was wider then Eleanor's but not as round. It jiggled as she walked to Tepus,

"I thought he would never sleep, that man only satisfies himself, that is why I need you, why I need this!" she said coyly as she kneeled down in front of Tepus taking his black spear in her hand.

Maggie was curious as to what was to happen. She knew they would have intercourse but just as the doggy-style was new to her this too seemed foreign. She never saw this before. It startled her as she saw Anne take the large black head into her mouth. Anne would lick and stroke Tepus. Maggie had never done that to Allan in her life. She thought it disgusting perhaps that is why Anne was satisfying Allan. She would perform orally on him. However, this scene made it look natural as Anne's dark skinned hand took a hold of his black penis, her fingers not even touching because of his girth.

Maggie felt a warmth in her crotch. Watching her friend had made her moist and this made her even more fidgety. She brought her skirt up to her waist, at first to cool herself then she put her fingers to her under garments to feel them. They were sticky and more liquid came forth the more she watched as Anne's wide ass wiggled, Tepus moaned "oooo you're so good at this" as he smiled at her. She too smiled at his approval. he moaned and moaned until he spewed his seed on her mouth and into her black curly hair. the gobs of it laid there in her rich locks.

Maggie found her fingers stroking herself. She had never done such a thing yet it felt right. She too was sweating and she watched as Anne stood up and positioned herself above, Tepus' large cock. She then turned around and Tepus' strong hands grabbed ahold of Anne's wide buttocks. His hands kneading them like dough. "That should be my ass in his hands, mine is so much better...." Maggie thought to herself as she ran her fingers around her inner lips.

Then Maggie's fingers stopped, all her concentration was on Anne's pussy. She watched in horror and envy as Anne lowered herself onto Tepus' black spear. It stretched her pussy to no end, Her lips clung to his penis as she stood up and came back down upon his penis. She would rotate her hips letting his penis come in and out just a bit. After several minutes she turned around on his massive tool. They kissed passionately as she wrapped her legs around him and he rose in the air. He positioned the town whore on her back and began to thrust into her with animalistic fury.

Maggie's fingers were rubbing her pussy vigorously, almost mashing it in frustration as she watched Anne's breasts bounce like water. Maggie then began to moan in an unknown sensation. Anne too was moaning like a mad woman. Maggie bit down on her free arm as she wanted to scream and a wave of pleasure rushed over her. She never knew such a thing. Her insides spasmed and she laid there in a sweaty heap watching down at the two lovers still going at it.

Never had she experience such a rush of sexual pleasure. Anne and Tepus too were experiencing their own pleasures. Maggie's eyes would widen when Tepus would furiously pound Anne and he would slip out exposing his enormous, wet, shiny weapon. Maggie counted twice that Anne would roll her eyes upward and kick her heels into his back screaming. Maggie assumed this to be some form of rush like she experienced. He would grunt and moan, and as his breath quickened the town whore said, "wait are you near your end?"

He nodded yes and she said, "please no, a black child would mean my death." Tepus then answered back, "Then let me leave my seed in your ass."

"NEVER!" Anne said. It was surprising that the town whore would not perform that service. Tepus then withdrew and in a rage shot his seed all over her belly and onto her breasts. Tepus then just walked away still hard and went to bed.

Maggie felt sorry for Tepus. Such a magnificent man. A body or rock and an incredible gift, and he wastes it on women who do not completely satisfy him. He pleasures them yet they do not fulfill his wish. They were not even beautiful enough to share in his masculinity, she thought to herself.

Anne simply got up and walked out the door. Maggie did notice that Anne was walking differently. It could still be seen how Tepus had stretched the town whore to the max.

Maggie fell asleep up there in the hay and awoke the next morning. Tepus had gone off to do his chores and Anne quickly made it back to the castle. She had not gotten her revenge but she learned many new things that night.

***

Anne looked at herself in her mirror as she sat naked in her chair. She moved in different positions wondering why she was so ugly. Why would Allan

228

choose to fuck a slut rather than her? How did Elaine win such a physically perfect man as Tepus.

Maggie stood up and put one of her long slender legs on the chair and she looked at her pussy. Its trim blonde hair and its tights lips. She wondered how they would look while a monstrous penis like Tepus' made her lips cling it to it like Anne's had.

Maggie turned around and looked at her flawless bubble butt. She squatted up and down and looked her flexed quads as she lowered herself up and down simulating the sex scenes she had seen the night before.

"Why are they so happy? All of them, Anne and Elaine are content. Allan is just fine with his pig-self. Yet I am empty and...." Maggie thought to herself.

She then remembered the look on Tepus' face last night. As he pleasured those women, they wouldn't satisfy him completely and he always looked so frustrated. Maggie then realized that she was not the only one unhappy with this whole situation.

All of these new revelations had gotten to the princess. Tonight was to be the grand ball and all types of men would be there trying to woo the princess. Perhaps she would use this opportunity to even the score with Allan.

That night Maggie prepared and dressed without the aid of Eleanor. She sent her on some errand and told her to stay home. She didn't want to face her after watching her being satisfied by Tepus. She dressed herself in her best dress. She wanted to attract attention to herself that night. As if she needed any assistance.

***

The music seemed to fill the hall and many of the guests were dancing. However, almost everyman's eyes stopped to watch the young princess walk in. A perfect vision of loveliness. Her massive breasts and firm buttocks were accentuated by the dress. It was simple yet constructive in how it enhanced every shape and contour of her body. Maggie knew she looked good and intended to use this as she shunned Allan when he approached her. She immediately went to a handsome knight and began to dance with him. All night she would dance with any man but Allan. She would feel their hardness pressed against her. Two or three had impressed her with their girth however, none really compared to Tepus. Still she would use their attention to get at Allan.

As the night wore on a bit Maggie excused herself from her current company. A prince from a far kingdom who had hoped to marry Maggie some time ago. As she walked towards the food a hand grabbed her arm and pulled her to the side.

"Allan! What has gotten into you!" she said assertively.

"Me? what about you. You prance around in that dress and dance with all the men but me? Let me remind you that I am your fiancée. Not these men you are consorting with like some common slut!"

The fire in his eyes scared her. His words stung her more. Slut? her? Fiancée? He was the one cheating on her with the town whore. She had been faithful to him for those years he was gone. God knows how many women he had in that time. And he had the gall to approach and reprimand her. The man she had once loved was really just a pig. All those years she had waited for his return. She was the princess who had her pick of any man and he looked at her like some filthy piece of garbage.

The emotions welled up inside her. Tears began to form around her round eyes, and still he stood there like a cold statue. It was too much for her too bear. She turned around and ran out a side door. Allan didn't want to make a scene and went back to the ball.

***

Maggie was now sobbing loudly as she walked about the outside of the castle. Most of the commoners were asleep and in their huts at this time

231

of night. She wandered a bit trying to wipe her tears. Off in the nearby distance she could hear someone with a deep voice talking. However it seemed they were talking to no one, and poorly at that. Maggie feared it was some illiterate lunatic. Who would be out in the streets at this time of night? Besides herself of course. She looked around and saw Allan's barn. The light was on. Perhaps she could see if Tepus would protect her.

As she ran in she realized the voice she heard was Tepus'. He was sitting on some hay. It appeared he was trying to read a book, suddenly he looked up to see the radiant princess in her amazing gown.

"To what do I owe this amazing pleasure?" he asked quizzically.

"Oh I was at the ball, and was having a wretched time. Was that you I heard reading?" she said as she approached him.

He sat upright on the bale of hay and put the book in his lap. It was a book from Allan's study. "Ummm, That was me. Although I don't read well. I speak English but I have been trying to understand the written words. It seems most people here are illiterate and have been no help to me."

"Well I'd be glad to help you." Maggie said as her eyes were now drying.

"It is much appreciated. Are you sure you won't get into any trouble? It seems most people that can read wouldn't help me because of my skin. I wouldn't want to endanger you."

He was worried about her. However truth be told, should anyone have caught him with the princess in a barn he wouldn't live past 5 seconds past that moment.

"I'd be glad to help you Tepus. It seems I have nothing better to do." she said taking a seat next to him.

"let's see what you can read now" she asked as Tepus opened the large tome with his long fingers.

"This tiiiime, wus the bist" he stammered.

"Oh that is a difficult part why don't you try reading this to begin." Maggie said caringly as she grabbed his hand and pointed to a particular sentence.

She had grabbed his hand only to guide it to the word however their touch send a jolt of electricity through both of them. They both looked at each other wide eyed and feeling a bit guilty they looked back at the words on the page.

Tepus began to read the elegantly hand written text.

"They weren't too sssssssuure...."

Maggie giggled a bit, "No Tepus, that word is sure. That must be pronounced like shhh at the beginning."

"Sssss" he struggled to spit out. He couldn't quite form the pronunciation.

"No, like this silly." She exclaimed as her two fingers pinched his bottom lip.

"Shhhhure. c'mon try it Tepus."

"Ssssss....."

"C'mon shhhhhure."

as they both worked at his pronunciation Maggie was unknowingly pulling her face closer to his as she too exaggerated her bottom lip coming out.

"Shure."

"Sssssure."

"C'mon just a bit shhure."

"Sssssssshure"

"Almost shure shure shure."

"Shure."

Just as he pronounced the word correctly, their lips met. Both of their eyes closed. Not thinking about who the other one was. His large lips almost enveloping hers as slowly their lips moved then their tongues began to dance on each other's.

Maggie slowly moaned as her hand was no longer pinching his lips but caressing his masculine face. Her other hand rested on his leg. His one hand was supporting him as his other gently caressed her golden tresses from her face. then slowly his hand then touched her arms, sides, until it rested on her hip. Rubbing his hand up and down her firm thighs. Her hand was now on his hip as she was balancing herself.

They stopped suddenly, both breathing hard. Maggie's enormous orbs bobbed up and down as she breathed heavily. Looking into Tepus' eyes. Tepus looked at hers as he too caught his breath. He brought his hand from her hip and wiped his bottom lip. Their eye contact stayed constant.

Suddenly a noise came. Someone was shouting from the castle's towers. They no doubt were searching for Maggie. She looked at him wide eyed, a bit frightened at being caught and what had just transpired.

"I must go." she said almost seeking his approval.

"Go, then. Don't wait here any longer." He spoke with genuine concern. Most men would've tried to keep her there. He let her go and she returned to the ball a very short time later. She explained to her father the King she had felt a bit ill and all went well the rest of the night.

***

The next day Maggie awoke with a strange sensation. Although her experience with Allan was emotionally devastating she felt reenergized. The thought of Tepus and her experience last night gave her new sensations. She had been sweaty from her dreams that night and her unexpected actions the previous evening. She just wanted to go to her brook to spend the day. She took her bar of soap which was rare to acquire as only few people could afford such a luxury and went to that private brook.

She again tried to avoid Eleanor. She wondered if she and Tepus still met at night. How could she have done that with her friend's lover? As Maggie made her way to the brook at almost the same time from a far end of the brook Tepus appeared. They waved too each other and soon met near some of the large rocks.

"Good to see you, I hope no harm found you last night." he said to her looking at her eyes.

235

"No I was quite alright. I just came here to bathe, I brought my soap and thought I would use it this one time."

"Soap?" Tepus quizzically asked.

"Yes it froths with water on your skin to help clean. I awoke in such a sweat from last night I thought this might be a fine time to use it." She said looking at his rags which were soaked.

"Yes I too was filthy with sweat. Allan found his book in the barn. He explained to me that such handwritten pieces cost quite a lot. He had me working hard most of this morning. I thought the water here would refresh me a bit. However, seeing as you are here I'll come back some other time. I'm sure you'd want the privacy for yourself."

Maggie felt saddened that he was going to leave, "Wait, you don't have to leave. We can bathe at the same time. The brook isn't that small you know."

Tepus turned around, "Yes but I'm sure you wouldn't want to bathe in your fine garments and these rags are all I have I must keep them dry for now."

Maggie thought of that for a moment, she wouldn't mind seeing Tepus and his well-defined body again. "Well then we can both bathe in the nude if wouldn't bother you."

Tepus was a bit surprised. "Are you sure, Maggie? I really could come back some other time."

"Oh no it's no trouble, after all I've seen you once here before. Perhaps now it would only be fair for you to see me."

Maggie would've never offered such a thing to another man. Only Allan had seen her naked and been with her at this brook. However Tepus was different.

Tepus slowly pulled his top over his head revealing his well-developed stomach and chest.

Maggie then removed her corset and top revealing her massive breasts. Which only lowered a bit and still stood firm and proud from her slight stomach and ribs.

They smiled at each other the entire time.

Tepus then removed his shoes and pants his massive tool waving back and forth between his legs.

Maggie then lowered her skirt. With her behind to him her muscular buttocks were exposed and as she bent over her meaty pussy poked through between her legs. As she stood, her strong legs exposed her quads and she turned around smiling as Tepus casually glanced at her trimmed golden pussy hair.

Maggie then took the soap in her hand and gave it to Tepus.

"After you."

Tepus then walked into the water till he was waist high in it. Maggie did the same. Both of their impressive chests just visible. The difference in the brooks floor was enough to make both their waists at the same level.

"Now Tepus submerge yourself and get yourself all wet. For the soap."

Tepus held his breath went down and came up. His head coming within inches of colliding with her proud breasts.

Maggie then too went down. As she went down she felt his massive tool floating in the water. She went down and felt it hit the bottom of her breasts and her rub across her angelic face. Then it even sat on her breasts a bit as she came up. She pulled her wet hair behind her.

Tepus then began to rub the bar on himself. It did little lathering.

"No, Silly. Here like this. Rub it in your hands once it lathers on your hands and do this."

Maggie's hand went on top of hers. She showed his fingers how to roll the bar until a nice lather appeared.

"Now apply it to your wet skin." she said as she guided his hand to his firm chest. The white suds contrasting against his skin as she guided his hand about his firm abs and pecs.

Their eyes met and that sexual tension began to mount again. "Is this right?" He asked as he made his motions faster with her hand still on top of his. "Perhaps you could lather my back then?" he asked. Maggie gladly obliged as he turned. She took her time to feel all his back muscles in her palm. She even looked at his bubble like butt which showed a bit at the water. She reached under the water to even lather those buns of his. They were different than most men. Most white men had relatively flat asses.

"Now you can do me." She said as she turned around grabbing her hair and pulling it in front of her over her right shoulder. Tepus took the soap from her hands and lathered up her smooth shoulders and arching back. He took his time rubbing small circles on her back. Maggie held onto her hair and closed her eyes as she moaned a bit. She moaned more as Tepus then Massaged her buttocks with lather underneath the water just as she had done for him. She would've said something but remembered it was only fair.

His hands came up again this time on her sides. His large hands and long fingers almost encircled her slim waist. He moved his hands to her front a bit feeling her rigid stomach muscles. He then moved up a bit and his fingertips were just making contact with her breasts. She then moved her bent arms over his hands and pulled him a bit closer to herself as she continued moaning softly. She felt his large penis just nestling a bit between her tight butt cheeks. She loosened them to allow his penis a warmer place to rest.

"Is that enough lather?" Tepus asked, his mouth close to her ears as he spoke softly.

"No, you still need the front." she said turning around. Her breathing making her large breasts stand proud. Her firm nipples were pointed in the air, further than they ever had before. He broke the bar into two pieces and put one into each hand. He lathered it up. Maggie put her hands on his as they rotated the soap. She guided his hands to each breast. Tepus gently applied the soap. Her nipples were so hard they hurt as he glided over them, around them, past them. She moaned more. Her right hand stopped his and took that piece of the bar from it as she then started to lather up his rippled front side. They gently caressed each other's fronts using their free hands to splash water upon each other to rinse off the soap and grime.

They both didn't know how far this would carry and Tepus asked "How much lathering would be enough?" he asked this to determine whether or not this would carry on to the next level.

"Well, I'm sure our legs deserve just as much attention." Maggie said. She grabbed his hand and guided him toward a rock which slanted slightly towards the water.

"Go ahead Tepus you first." she said watching him as he rose from the water. His triceps flexing as he hoisted his strong body onto the rock. He put one foot upon the rock and another still in the water. His long penis lying alongside the leg still flaccid. It hadn't shrunk like most other men. His wet, black skin shone in the sun. Maggie took the soap and carefully washed his calves and thighs. Her hands avoiding his penis. Until she grabbed the massive black cock in her hand. She squeezed it to get a grip and wondered at how soft it was and its massive girth. She lifted it up to wash his leg underneath. Then she washed it carefully. Applying soap along its length. She even pulled back on the foreskin exposing the massive head which made Tepus moan and brought her back to reality. She was so enthralled with his penis she forgot about the man attached to it. She then soaped his enormous testicles.

Not wanting to seem like a whore Maggie remembered the reason for this. "There you go Tepus. Now just slide into the water and you'll be nice and fresh."

"That did feel quite good. However I suppose it's fair you get a turn now." he said as he jumped into the water. The suds floated about the top of the water. He then waded to Maggie and picked her up and placed her gently upon the rock. Her breasts were gleaming and her trim golden pubic hair glistened with beads of water. Maggie began to feel a moistness inside herself. As Tepus took his time and washed her feet. His long fingers sliding between her toes. Taking extra time so as to massage them yet not tickle them. She threw her head back as his fingers not only soaped up but massaged her tight calves. His strong hands enveloped her thighs. He soaped up her hamstrings and quads and then as he reached her upper thigh his hand guided the soap about her small tuft of pubic hair. His palm touching her inner folds. This caused her to shudder as she looked down. His black skin contrasting against her white skin. Their muscular bodies shining with wetness. Tepus then began soaping her inner thighs with his one hand while his other hand slowly went over her pussy lips.

The sensation was near orgasmic. She had never felt anything like that. As Tepus moved in a bit and his face approached her eager slit. His hot breath was amazing as his fingers began to gently move about her mound. While her body was devoid of any fat. Her tempting mound certainly was thick with sudden need. Tepus moved his hands about her warm skin. His hot breath was almost breathing fire into her.

A woman's voice came from the woods, "Magdelina are you there?"

It was Eleanor! She couldn't see Maggie like this. Maggie immediately sat up and she was practically sitting on Tepus face and shoulders.

"Quickly, into the water!" she said as her weight went upon him and he fell into the water. She was waist high into it when she felt his mouth on her privacy. She was about to die from the feeling. His tongue had begun working on her insides and her strong thighs clamped about his head.

Eleanor emerged from the woods, "Come quickly Maggie, Everyone's been looking for you!!!!!! Hurry!"

Maggie found her senses and quickly got out of the water, grabbed her clothes and quickly got dressed. Then she followed the running Eleanor. Maggie looked back just to see Tepus arise from the water. His knees submerged and his penis hanging there as he waved to her. Maggie waved back and followed Eleanor.

***

"The county will soon be under attack my lord." an aide told the King. His daughter had just rushed in. "What is it father?" she Asked quite breathless.

The king said, "Our kingdom may come under attack within the next few days. We have word of renegade forces approaching. They currently are attacking Galecia. I want you to stay within the castle for the time being. No more scurrying about. It is too dangerous."

Maggie was saddened and realized this house imprisonment might endanger her chances of being with Tepus again. Although she wasn't thinking of sexual escapades she longed to see him or share time with him. "but father....."

He quickly interrupted her, "That is final. Your all I have little flower. Since I lost your mother I cannot lose you. Please it's just for your own safety. Hopefully the renegades will pass us by and we can resume our lives."

Maggie knew he was simply being a father and she agreed. She went to her special room in the tower and looked upon the castle and town that had ever been her home. She was worried for her father's safety and the kingdom's. She hoped no harm would come she also wondered when she would see Tepus again.

***

Maggie's whole day was spent in the tower. Allan tried to contact her and come to her room but she refused him access. Telling her guards to not let him even come to the stairway's entrance. Eleanor came by and the two talked into the wee hours of the night. Eleanor eventually had to leave and Maggie's mind had to wonder if she was off to a late night hook up with Tepus. She was angry at Eleanor and realized that those two were having a relationship. Although it seemed purely sexual.

A bit after one of the guards knocked on Maggie's door.

"What is it?" she asked as she put her nightgown on for the evening.

The guard replied, "It's sir Allen's slave......."

her ears perked up

"he says he has a message from him. since it's not Sir Allen should I allow him to deliver it? If he makes one wrong move I can kill the moor if you want."

Maggie tried to hide her excitement. "Let him in, he's no threat."

The guard led Tepus up the stairs and let him in the door. Tepus handed Maggie a note on some paper that seemed crudely written. Maggie looked at the guard, and said, "Some privacy please. I wish to convey a message back to Allan." The guard looked mad and puzzled at the same time. Leaving the princess alone with this savage not only endangered her but his job and life too. Nevertheless he obeyed her command.

As the door slammed shut Maggie put the note on her nightstand. The candlelight illuminating her voluptuous figure underneath her almost sheer white nightgown.

"I enjoyed the bath today. The soap was rejuvenating." Tepus said straight-faced.

"Yes, it was quite invigorating." Maggie said with a shy smile. "Did Allan really send you?"

"No I used it to get past the guards. Unless you don't want me here." Tepus said ready to turn around to the door.

"Oh no, I was actually..." she stopped her words to go to the door, she slightly opened it to check that the guard went all the way back down the steps. "hoping to see you." Her bending around the door opening had given Tepus quite a show and her nightgown did nothing to hide her now erect nipples. When she turned around and leaned back against the door she could see Tepus' ragged pants rising. She had seen his penis flaccid many a time but in arousal was rare.

"I too wanted to thank you. For helping me wash up." she finished her sentence.

He walked to her and smelled her hair, "Yes your as fragrant as ever." as she nestled her blonde hair against his chest. Her hard nipples and firm breasts pressing into his body causing his penis to stir more. As it rose she took hold of it with her left hand. As it began to harden she could not get a grip on it. Her slender fingers getting a workout. She smelled him too. He reeked of total manliness.

"You smell good as well." She said rubbing her cheeks against him smelling him as her hand stroked him through his pants. She slipped her hand into his pants and lifted his amazing tool out of those rags. Its length appeared incredible when up so close. She could almost lift it to her head and she bent down a little and smelled it. She lowered herself to her knees and looked at is as she slowly pulled the foreskin back on its enormous head. For some reason, his half-hard penis looked so smooth and soft. She took it into her mouth and tasted him for the first time. She began to gently suckle on it. She had never done such a thing yet this seemed natural.

Tepus leaned his head back and groaned. For a first time Maggie could sense she was giving him pleasure. She stroked his penis with both hands as she repeatedly would have the big head POP in and out of her mouth. He was hardening and his large girth was proving to be a challenge. Tepus moved her hair from her face as her breathing was getting frantic trying to take all of him into her mouth. Tepus leaned down and took his dick from her mouth. He lifted her in the air his black spear standing in front of him. He lifted her to the bed where he laid her down. As she knelt next to his cock and took him to her mouth, he surprised her as he grabbed her hips and placed her strong ass near his head and lifted up her nightgown. Exposing her silky privates to him.

She was caught off guard momentarily and the sensation of his lips near her pussy again was incredible. His hot breath was killing her as he gazed at her meaty pussy. His large lips meeting hers. He began to expertly eat her out. As her sensations increased her oral pace on his cock increased. She did all that she could to excite him. Quickly a sudden rush came over her. Something new. It emanated from her groin and washed over her in pleasure as it seemed Tepus' tongue had touched something special inside of her. She paused for several minutes breathing hard. She had realized that was the first great pleasure of her life and she was hell bent on repaying him. She worked on his penis again as he worked on her again. Suddenly his penis throbbed in her mouth just as her loins throbbed too. Just as the next sensation hit her she wanted to scream but his penis began to shoot semen into her mouth. It tasted warm and good and she swallowed as much as she could her own orgasm making her moan.

They both groaned so loud the guard began to make his way to the room. They both heard his steps and Maggie quickly tried rubbing his semen into her dress as he wiped his wet face and covered himself with his rags. The guard opened the door just as Tepus began to walk out. Maggie laid herself on her bed. The guard looked about and proceeded to lead Tepus down the stairs. Maggie laid back in bed exhausted. As she licked her sticky fingers. She looked at her nightstand and read the note Tepus had brought. It said, Thank You, For Teaching Me To Read. Is this good?

"Oh it's good Tepus, and thank you for teaching me something." She thought to herself.

Part 3

Maggie opened her eyes to the warm sunshine. A warmth was coming from her insides as she stretched. She felt like a new person. Last night with Tepus had taken their relationship from innocent flirtation to a new level. A level of sexual exploration she could have never imagined ever having with any man. Her smile was stretching across her angelic face when a knocking on her door made her sit up.

Allan then busted into the room.

"Is it true! Was my moor slave here in your room last night?" He bellowed with a furious look on his face.

"Yes." Maggie weakly answered. Did he know what happened? How could he?

"How dare he? I'll have him hanged as soon as I return to my quarters!" Allan said seeing the shamed look on Maggie's face.

Maggie then realized what he was saying. Was he accusing her of an affair? Even if he was right, what right did he have to make such an accusation? She was the most beautiful woman in the land and the king's daughter no less. She was a prize for the entire country and perhaps Europe.

"Listen here you smug pig! He was here trying to tell me how apologetic you were and that you felt sorry for offending me. He was trying to help you! How dare you want to hang your own slave!" She angrily screamed, pointing her finger into his chest.

"He did?" Allan asked, curious as to why Tepus would do such a thing for him. He then realized the situation and wanted to take advantage of it. Feeling aroused seeing Maggie in her night clothes...."Well of course. I'm terribly sorry Maggie. He was right, I have been wrought with grief."

Maggie saw right through him and saw him for what a pig he truly was. He smiled at her, content with his new position and saw him leering at her chest.

"Allan, I wish not to see you right now. Perhaps you should leave." She told him while turning away.

He walked up behind her and pulled her close. She felt his little penis through his pants and she angrily shoved him away. "Leave now! Lest I call the guards." As she pointed to the door. Like a dog with his tail between his legs, Allan made his way down the stairs and out of the castle. Maggie went to wash herself from last night's activities. Sweat and semen had made her feel a bit unclean, or perhaps it was Allan's unexpected appearance that gave her that feeling.

Maggie began to call for her maid and wanted to draw herself a bath. Then the warm brook popped into her head. Perhaps she would see Tepus. Perhaps she could.....well other things began to pop into her head. It was amazing how such a sexually timid woman had been transformed recently. No less without even having sexual relations with a man. At least not the traditional kind.

Maggie dressed in a thick dress and wrapped her head in a cloth covering to conceal herself. She snuck herself out of the castle and towards the woods, making her way to the brook.

As she began to high step through the tall grass in her thick concealing garb something knocked the princess down. She looked up as two men on horseback jumped off their horse and grabbed her by the arm.

"What have we got here, John?" the taller of the two said, through gritted yellow teeth.

"Seems a leper, and a trespasser. This here area be forbidden leprous bitch." he said leering close but wary of what he thought was a leper.

"Damn shame, seems she got quite a set on her. If they fall off I might have to mount them on my wall." he said as he grabbed and squeezed her breast. They both laughed when suddenly their horse ran off startled. There was a rustling in the grass. They looked as another rock landed in the grass. The distraction worked as a man flew from nowhere. A fist landed on the taller one's chin sending him flailing to the ground. John, was tackled to the ground and was met with some fists to his own face.

Maggie tried to get up but fell back down as an immense pain shot through her ankle. Maggie then looked as she brushed her hair and cloths from her face and saw that it was Tepus fighting these two men.

The taller one returned to his feet and jumped on Tepus' back. They wrestled back and forth as

John tried to regain his bearings, his nose bloody and tooth missing. Maggie saw that the horse was nearby and whistled to it. Her years of horse riding made her quite the animal person. The horse came and she struggled to get on top of it. As she did she saw that Tepus had started to beat on the taller man however, John had gotten to his feet and pulled out a dagger. Maggie rushed the horse to Tepus and screamed, "Tepus c'mon!"

Maggie slowed the horse a bit and Tepus jumped onto its backside as John lunged at Tepus' back with the knife. Missing Tepus he lunged into his tall friends shoulder. John watched his friend scream in pain as Tepus clutched the horse's backside, feet dragging along the ground. He pulled himself atop the horse and grabbed around the waist of this mystery rider. "Thank you." he told her. "No thank you, I owe you much more."

Tepus was curious as to who this was. Their heavy breathing made it no simpler to recognize her voice. "May I ask how you knew my name?" Tepus asked. Maggie pulled her hood down and looked back at him. "By the eternal, this is unexpected. If you go towards the hills I know a spot we can rest." He informed her.

The hills went past the brook, which Maggie was looking forward too. However, the person she was looking for had made it. Even though their meeting was a bit impromptu.

***

Tepus pointed out the destination to Maggie. There was an opening in the large face of the

251

woods. It was small and it seemed some kind of connection allowed her to see what he spoke of. He didn't have to point it out to her, only mention it. The horse galloped in the correct direction. The wooded area seemed a bit familiar to Maggie.

Tepus spoke to her softly. "I've been wanting to show you this for a long time, there is a trail I roughly made, follow it."

Again their unspoken bond seemed to guide Maggie upon the trail. The trail led to the top of a hill, which gave a sparkling view of a brook. It was their brook.

"Oh my I've never seen this view!" Maggie exclaimed, watching the sun reflect off the angles of the water.

"It is beautiful isn't it?" Tepus observed, leaning close, his strong chest against her back.

They both heard a splashing and looked around. It was Anne and Eleanor. Splashing around naked. Their giggles could be heard but they're conversation could not.

"Who needs that moor? Black bastard!" Anne the town whore remarked, bringing back her long hair with her two arms, causing her large tits to bounce as she eyed up the lean glistening frame of Eleanor.

Eleanor's small perky breasts and nipples were excited as she embraced Anne's soft body. Their lips meeting in a passionate kiss as their hands roamed each other's hips and sides.

Eleanor walked back and leaned against the same edge Maggie had once laid her back upon.

Now Anne was taking Tepus' place and was beginning to eat from Eleanor's lithe body.

Anne's experienced tongue now worked on young Eleanor, her lean legs moving about, her perky tits being tugged at with her own hands.

Anne then climbed upon the rock, positioning herself to 69 her newfound friend as the two new lesbians enjoyed each other's taste. Eleanor's hands reached and fondled Anne's large breasts as they hung down. Their tongues going deeper and deeper into each other.

The paces of the observer's breathing had quickened as they watched the exhibition down below them. Tepus was looking over Maggie's shoulder and the closeness of their bodies allowed them to know each other's breathing had grown heavy, as well as the now rapid beating of their hearts. Maggie could feel Tepus' hot breath on her neck and his manhood was hardening at the sight of the lady lovers going at it.

As exciting as this revelation was, it came to Maggie with a heavy heart. She then remembered the relationship Tepus had with these two. She suddenly became proud that, as far as she had gone with Tepus he had never had her completely. It was then that Tepus turned his head, suggesting... "Let's go, leave these two be alone."

Maggie retorted, "Why, wish you could join them?"

"Those two? Never again. I turned them away, and they've threatened me. They'll claim that I've raped them. I have no fear of Anne. Who will believe the town whore unless she speaks to your man, Allan. Eleanor, I know doesn't have the heart to do such a thing. It's a threat of serious proportions, yet I cannot love them ever again."

His answer came with fear and confidence. Maggie knew he was right, and the connection between Anne and Allan still troubled her greatly as she gazed intently on the writhing female bodies below.

"Maggie?" Tepus asked trying to attract her attention

"Yes......" her voice trailing off, her mind filled with so many emotions at the moment.

"Can we leave? I'd rather not watch this. I have something even more special I'd like to show you." Tepus said.

The trail led them to yet another opening in the thick woods. It was a vast field of flowers. Maggie recognized it from her childhood, she hadn't been there in years.

"I remember this field, oh how beautiful it's grown!" she explained, Staring at the various colors of flowers.

"As soon as I saw this place, I thought of you." Tepus remarked in a saddened tone, almost ashamed about letting his feelings show a bit.

Maggie began to blush, she too was embarrassed a bit by what he had said. She still had no idea what to make of Tepus. They had obviously experienced something together, however she wondered if she was just another woman to him, much like Anne and Eleanor were, and as she seemed to her fiancée Allan. She needed to sort out her feelings. Tepus grew nervous at the silence.

"How is your injury? Do you think the castle guards will be looking for you?"

"Yes, my injury seems to be a bit better. They must miss me at the castle. I've been gone awhile." she too said in a hushed saddened tone.

Without speaking any more words, they headed back towards the castle. Maggie also remembered that she now had to sneak into the castle just as she had snuck out of it.

The horse drew close to the castle walls, Maggie began to cover herself more in her costume hiding her identity. "Oh, if my father finds that I have left, he'll have my head." she said with certainty.

"Then let me help you sneak in." Tepus offered.

"Oh I couldn't let you do that, besides I have a secret way into the castle. It's been long since I've used it, but I'm sure it's ways are still open." Maggie told him, smiling into his eyes. She was thankful for his chivalry.

"Yes, but the potential for your capture is there. I wouldn't want you to displease your father and lose favor with him. Especially not for me, since I'm the reason you've been kept out so long." Tepus said, her smile warming him inside.

"Really, Tepus I'll be fine. It's an old hallway. Quite a maze in there, but I'll get through alright." Maggie said turning away.

"I won't let you go alone. Not that I doubt your memory, you could get lost Maggie. I'd hate for that to happen. After all, who will teach me to read?"

A smile crossed both their faces.

Tepus continued, "besides, if they catch me with you. They'll punish me a bit more and I can take the blame."

"Don't be silly, Tepus. I enjoyed my time with you." She said, her hand holding his arm. Her eyes travelled to her hand. The sun light gave the horizon an orange glow as she looked into his handsome face. She wasn't sure of what she was about to say, but it seemed to come from her with no hesitation.

"Well, the last time we were in the castle it was quite an experience. Plus, I'd hate to run into some of those guards. You know they do look at me in the most unflattering ways."

With that they moved along the fortifications until they found a crack in the wall. They both squeezed into the small crevice. Maggie had a minor problem as her breasts and buttocks had grown a bit since the last time she had to sneak into the castle after playing late with the village children. They then dropped to the ground and crawled a bit through a narrow passageway. Tepus followed Maggie the whole time. Even under her supposed "leper covering" rags her buttocks moved as though it was mimicking her original movements. Tepus hardly complained until they hit the opening.

A hallway opened up. Not completely dark as the setting sun seemed to illuminate the hallway a bit through cracks in the decrepit walls. Tepus had to slouch his tall frame a bit to walk the small hall. The lack of light was becoming a problem as they walked.

"This hallway existed as a further extension of this castle. They decided against that plan before I was even born and it was never used. I used to run here as a kid when I had to hide from my caretakers or sneak back inside." She said with a sly grin.

"Never one for your castle are you?" Tepus asked.

"Not that I hate my living. I loved my upbringing, I know I've been blessed, but sometimes I long for a true friend though. There are so many artificial people within these castle walls." Maggie explained as they continued to walk.

"How many of these halls are there like this?" Tepus asked, the hall seeming to lower even more.

"Several along the east and southern walls. This one will end shortly, then we'll have to run through a large hall that is still in use. It's near the dungeon. Past the large hall is another crack to another unused hall, that one has a slope which leads to a spot where I can remove some blocks and be upon the spiral staircase, which leads directly to my room." Maggie softly explained to him as they approached the end of the current hallway. Maggie pulled back a small lever which opened a small entry about ten large bricks in size. He seemed to move the brick laden panel quite easily.

"Have you ever shown your beloved this way before?" Tepus asked as he tried his best to be as stealthy as possible.

Maggie gave a puzzled look to Tepus. Was he insinuating something between them, how she wished it was but she remembered about him and the other women. She even cursed herself still a bit about the night in her room, even at the brook.

"Wh..wh..." she stammered until he eased her fears or diminished her hopes.

"I mean Allan." He said in a soft voice.

"Oh never..." her voice trailed off as she peeked out of the crevice. The coast was clear.

"I must leave you here now Tepus or you'll never find your way back thank you for the wonderful day." Maggie said quickly. Giving Tepus a slight peck on the cheek then turning to get out of the crack.

She got out and started running towards the next hidden entrance. As she looked back she saw Tepus behind her, shutting the secret brick door.

"I don't want to leave you." He said, as he quickly followed her.

"Well you didn't come here for no reason. Quick! Help me." she spoke quietly, her slender fingers searching to remove the years of dirt from the loose bricks she once knew were there.

His hands covered hers as his fingers worked quickly to move the bricks and they crawled through the small hole they had made, he then turned and pulled the bricks back into place as best he could.

"Well the hard part is done isn't it?" He said a bit out of breath from the hurried excavation.

"Not exactly," she grinned. "Now I have to remember where the secret passages are. This hall has many, and I don't remember exactly where all of them are or where they lead too."

They both looked at each other knowing their predicament and shared a chuckle.

"Well then, I might have to get something." Tepus said. He then turned around and slightly pushed out the bricks. He slid out of the hallway. Maggie looked at the opening in fear of what he had planned and then a torch from the hall was handed to her through the opening. Tepus then followed it.

"Might need some light, It seems a bit dark in here." He said taking hold of the torch.

"Good thinking, glad I don't have to do all the work here." Maggie said playfully.

They walked down a hallway and took several turns. All the while, Maggie hoped to remember where she was going. Most of it seemed familiar to her. Thankfully, they came to the slope. It was a tall slope that had to be crawled into and would then lead to the bricks along the spiral staircase that led to her room. It was a relief to see the slope although something nagged at her.

The two began to slowly crawl the slope. Maggie all the while trying to remember something. There was something about this slope that she had forgotten. What was it? She was sure it led to her spiral staircase. So if she was headed for the staircase then she knew there could be no more surprises. Then it came to her, or she came to it.

As she put the heels of her palms upward and her weight on the slope it gave as though a trap door would on a floor. She tumbled downward and Tepus who had been following closely behind watching her buttocks followed as well.

Their bodies rumbled down a chute, the fall was shorter than expected as they ended up in a heap. Fortunately the torch landed beside them on the ground, embers bouncing upon the cold hard stone.

The two looked around to what seemed an abandoned room. Maggie recognized it as her old play room. She had forgotten about the chute which she used to play with for endless hours. She felt silly for forgetting about it, but glad to see it again. Her old bed was gray from the dust that covered it. The sun light was angled right at the lone window in the room. Its light barely lit the place. Dust had risen from their sudden entrance.

Tepus then let another groan out and fell to his side.

"Oh my Tepus, are you alright. I'm sorry I didn't mean too!" she said, her hand on top of his as it clutched his side.

He looked up into her eyes, and said, "I thought angels had wings to soften their falls from the heavens."

She giggled through a pained face, fearing for him. She gathered her dust covered blanket from the bed and tossed it aside.

"Here lie here for now. Perhaps you'll feel better. After a bit." She said, helping him to rise and lie on the bed.

The torch's light mixed with the sun had given an amazing lighting to the room. Maggie gently stroked his pained face as she saw the sweat glisten of his rich, dark skin.

"Had I known there would be a visitor, I might have prepared this room a little better." she joked

"You planned that fall?" Tepus asked

"Oh no, I can't believe I forgot about that trap door. It's been years since I've been here." She replied in all sincerity.

"The result was unwelcome, but my present company surely is appreciated." Tepus said, smiling as his hand covered hers, his other holding his side.

Maggie smiled back, she was concerned for him. She hoped he hadn't broken anything on account of her.

"Let me see how bad it is?" She asked him as her slender white hand reached underneath his shirt. Her hands feeling his hard body underneath, he was as hard as the floor they had landed on. He removed his hand as her hand explored his ribs.

"Aaahhh, there it is." He exclaimed through clenched teeth.

"They do not feel broken, I'm so terribly sorry Tepus." Maggie said, her hands reluctantly, leaving his body.

"A small price to pay, to spend such time with you." Tepus said, his forehead wrinkled in pain. As he said this, his hand returned to his ribs. They covered Maggie's hand before she could remove hers. His thumb rubbing her hand.

Their eyes locked, Maggie asked Tepus. "Tepus, may I ask something of you?"

"Anything...." he answered her. He was ready to entrust his heart and soul to her.

"Anne and Eleanor, why did you turn them away?" Maggie said, her eyes almost begging Tepus to give her an answer to relieve her worries. To give her the permission to abandon herself to this man.

"They meant nothing to me....Eleanor she caught me at the brook just as you did, then she told that whore Anne. Anne had been forcing me to take her or she would accuse me of raping Eleanor. Eleanor, seemed to come after me with great fervor." He explained.

"You continued with them, why turn them away. What if Anne comes through on her threat?" Maggie asked, leaning closer to him, wanting to hear his answer.

"I've come to believe....hope no one will listen to Anne. Even if they kill me, I would rather have that, then to be their object of desire. Besides, I long ago came to the decision that there is only one that I want. One that I've wanted for so long, yet didn't know her name or what she looked like, until I met her." Tepus said with a true sense of honesty in his voice.

"And who would that be?" Maggie spoke in a breathless sigh. Her eye brows raised on her pure face. A look of hope upon her.

His hand left her hand, it brushed away her hair as he raised himself a bit. Biting his lip in pain.

"I cannot say, for her heart belongs to a man I must call master." Tepus said.

Her heart aching now in pain Maggie's hand held his upon her face.

"No man is your master, especially since I love no man save for one." She replied in desperation. Her body aching for his touch, for him.

Her hand stroking his, a long pause occurred as they stared deep into each other's eyes.

"And who would that be?" Tepus said with the same kind of hope and desperation in his voice as well.

Maggie could hold it no longer, "It's the man who's captured my imagination and had never done anything to hurt me. He's been nothing but true and honest. He's the one I've waited for, I thought I had met him and it wasn't Allan....it was......"

she paused, not sure whether to continue or not. By now their faces were so close to each other's, their eyes locked, any hesitation was killed by the look in his eyes as she continued.

"It's you Tepus, It always has been."

Part 4

Their lips met in an almost violent collision as their passions melted within each other's arms. Their hands roaming each other as they enjoyed the softness of each other's lips. Their tongues touching in beautiful coordination as Tepus struggled to sit up more, his hands in her hair and upon her hips. Her hands roaming his strong shoulders and arms.

Their kisses only breaking for chances to catch their breath. Sucking up air they exchanged professions of their love for each other.

"Oh I've longed for you for so long" Tepus said his kisses now exploring her lower neck as her hands roamed upon his head.

"I've wanted you more and more, I've begun to love you and it only grows with each passing moment" she exclaimed as her leg wrapped around his pulling him closer. His kisses now exploring her face and then sucking on her ear lobe as he rested his head on her shoulder holding her closer.

"No one has meant as much to me as you have, I've been lost since I've left my land, till I met you." Tepus said, their embrace parting as Maggie backed up. The silence could have been disheartening but the intense passion in the air between them only seemed to intensify in the dimly lighted room.

Maggie reached behind her head, removing the cloths that made the hood off her dress. Shaking her hair free of the collar of the dress, she looked at Tepus with fierce passion. Their faces expressionless save for their eyes, focused intently on each other.

Her hands reached under the bottom of his shirt, his hands raised as he helped her remove his shirt. The light bouncing of his ebony body. Hard and muscled, glistening like polished marble from his sweat. Maggie stood from the bed and turned her back to him.

She turned around her hair all to one side as she eyed him. She then bent over and kissed him hard and full on the lips as she reached about his pants and took them off. Tepus raised his buttocks from the bed, although in slight discomfort and let his pants fall to the ground. He lay there in his nakedness. The light casting shadows accentuating his rigid body and long, dark penis.

Still in her heavy dress Maggie kissed him again, her hand roaming his chest. She broke the kiss and pushed him back upon his elbows. She took a step back, looking at him with his buttocks slightly off the bed. His long thick shaft laying back against him, almost to his belly button.

She bunched her dress in her fist and she sat down upon one of his legs. She had not worn underwear and her pussy was covering his legs in her juices. She enjoyed the sensation of the little hairs on his leg as she leaned close to his face.

"Tepus, no man has made me want him this much. Tonight I want to give myself to you. All of myself, everything. My soul, my heart, and tonight I want to excite you to the limit." she said huskily, her fingers dragging across his chest as she began to rock her hips along his leg.

He sat up, his hands resting upon her knees and then traveling up and down, rubbing her strong thighs as she rocked back and forth on him. He kissed her neck and lips as she rocked harder and harder. Her arms wrapped about his head and pressed his face against her full, yet still covered tits. He tried to cover them with his mouth even though the cloth separated his mouth from her well-developed mounds. Her grip upon his head tightened as she began to press down even harder against his leg. His one hand found her pussy lips as she kept rocking more, begging for his intruding finger.

Her body then seemed to freeze and convulse at the same time as waves of pleasure washed over her. She released his head and his mouth now found hers again.

"Mmmm, Tepus you excite me to no end." She exclaimed, giggling. "As you do to me." He replied. Maggie looked down to see his thick member standing at half-mast. She stood off of his leg and turned around.

She bent down with her back to Tepus. Bent over, feet crossed one over the other, she began to pull the dress over her head. Tepus watched with a dry mouth as his heavy breathing continued.

She lifted her dress above well-formed tight calves, which led to milky smooth legs...ending upon a swelling of hips and a strong buttocks. As it slid upward, narrowing at a slim waist, the smooth arch of her back met her long blonde hair. She turned slightly to look at him.

His thick penis stood in the air at full attention. An obelisk to be worshipped, she turned around slowly to see him, his rich skin, hard muscles, and large member were offered for her.

He looked out of breath at his prize. Her long blonde hair framed angelic eyes and full lips, leading down a beautiful neck to two generous swells with amazing, pronounced nipples which actually cast a shadow. Her tits pointed down to a toned abdomen, trailing off to a light patch of cunt hair and strong legs.

Her legs were sexily flexing and her breasts bounced in amazing rhythm as she approached him. She stood between his legs, she stepped over his left leg with her right, he slid his ass off the edge of the bed more allowing her to step over his other leg. She sat down on his strong legs. Ass hanging in the air, her firm legs balancing her, pussy dripping upon his sack. She looked down to see his black spear up high against her own body.

"Are you ready for this?" Tepus asked in loving concern.

"More than anything in my life. I want us to happen," Maggie said with great love in her voice.

She stood up and Tepus could only watch in amazement. Her strong quads positioned her thick pussy above his phallus. Her pussy lips were full and felt amazing as they slowly made the head of his penis disappear. A small grunt escaping Maggie's lips.

"Oh my, more than I could've Imagined...."Maggie said, rotating her hips as she slowly worked her wet pussy onto Tepus

"Oh goodness..." Tepus hissed as the feeling of her tight wet pussy engulfed his member. Never had anything felt so warm and inviting in his life.

Maggie slowly worked, her breathing increasing. Tepus eyes her magnificent breasts as her lungs made them heave. The shadows her breasts cast accentuated her movements. They moved toward him as the muscles in her abdomen strained as she engulfed his massive rod. She slowly began to move up and down upon Tepus until she had reached the bottom.

His penis had completely entered her. They both stopped, Tepus with his arms on the bed, Maggie her hands on his knees as she reclined back to see the contrast of her white body upon his black body. Then with gentleness Tepus lowered himself and ever so slightly began to thrust himself up into Maggie.

Maggie had never had anything so large moving within her. Within a few strokes she grew accustomed to his size and she began to move and thrust her pussy a bit towards Tepus causing an amazing sensation. His manhood further exciting her with each thrust, her pussy motions were effecting him to no end as well. He had to have every inch of this fiery lady.

They both began to grunt in animalistic passion as Maggie was sitting above this amazing black man seemingly dancing as his black pole ascended into her. The dimly lit room seemed nothing but shadows, the light showing Tepus' sweaty abs help thrust his penis into her as her belly seemed to rotate, each muscle with a purpose as her movements were meant to excite her new lover.

Tepus hands ran along her sides, sometimes grabbing and covering her large full breasts. She held her hair in her hands as she danced upon his eager prick. Her legs felt weak from sheer passion. She came down totally on Tepus and wrapped her legs around his torso. Her hair covering Tepus face as she fell completely onto him. Their lips and tongues finding each other. The velvet feel of their tongues was only rivaled by the feeling of their bodies intertwined in each other. Tepus rolled her over and his hand underneath her grabbing her shoulders as he continued to fuck hard into this salacious woman.

"Oooooooooohhh Tepus, you monster. Ooooooooooo love me, don't stop don't.....aaaaiiiieeeeeeeee" Maggie screamed as Tepus could only moan.

"Uuuhhhhh Maggie.....Maggie Maggie......." He could only repeat her name as he entered into a warmth he could've only dreamt about. He lowered his head and played his tongue upon her full breasts as he entered her repeatedly. Nearing his climax he propped his arms about her head and raised himself. He began to pound Maggie increasing his pace. She encouraged him, her muscled legs drawing him closer, her hips meeting his every thrust. They both neared their ends and Maggie then threw her arms up and held onto him as tight as possible.

Crushing her huge chest against his, she held onto him. Her legs like a fleshy vice On his slender hips, his protruding buttocks clenched as his semen rushed out of him. His balls tightening as he filled Maggie with himself.

Maggie bit his shoulder to keep from screaming in indescribable passion, his mouth was speechless as his body reached a point he never had before. He toppled onto the bed, with Maggie atop him.

"Oh.......never in my life!" Tepus howled, looking at the ceiling

Weakly Maggie moved her hips a bit with his long penis still inside of her. It was still dribbling inside her.

"Me neither. Oh Tepus, that was amazing." She kissed his chin. He was finding his second wind very rapidly. Her shapely warmth worked his penis quite rigid once more. Those amazing breasts moved across his chest. His need grew quickly as their lips met again.

He grabbed her in a hug as they kissed and began to thrust once more into this now cum soaked princess. Easily sliding into her she broke the kiss. Placing her hands on his shoulder raising her chest to his mouth as he greedily sucked upon her breasts. She then proceeded to turn away and let his dick totally reenter her. She rode his penis as he could only watch her amazing ass move as she clenched it, moving around and around upon his thick phallus.

Tepus' watching her body only brought about the animal in him as his arm wrapped around her abdomen. He pushed her forward onto the bed and held onto her slim waist and occasionally rubbing her thick hips, he took her from behind. His grunting growing louder and louder.....Until Maggie stopped him.

She turned around and pushed him down. She mounted him and held her hands upon his wrists. He could easily overpower her but she was in control. She slowly rubbed her pussy upon his thick cock as her breasts hung in front of his face. Without the aid of her hands she arched her hips and slid his thick head into her warm pussy with animalistic need.

"Mmmmmmm, my love....how is this..."Maggie asked him as she worked his member. She clenched her pussy about him when she pulled up on his cock.

As his cock began to throb she quickly raised off his cock and stuffed his half hard penis into her mouth. She greedily sucked and teased his head with her tongue until he came. She clamped her mouth and beautiful lips upon his black cock until he had spouted into her mouth. His sweet taste invaded her mouth as she whole-heartedly swallowed almost every drop.

She then slowly climbed up his muscled black body and rested her head on his chest as the torch finally died out leaving the room in dimness.

***

271

After the tryst, she told him she wanted to see him again and explained to him how he could get out of the secret room area. She quietly proceeded to her room so as not to arouse any suspicions. The next morning, a loud commotion awoke the princess in her room.

Maggie threw on a gown as she ran about the castle looking to see what the hustle was about. She then saw Allan.

"Ahh my love thank god your safe." he said to her.

"What are you talking about Allan?" Maggie asked him in a bit of a fury.

"We found the moor in your old playroom! He was lying there asleep and naked. He could've raped you. You know those beasts and their lust for white women." Allan growled

"Noooo....." Maggie said in horror as she saw down the hall they were leading Tepus down to the dungeon.

"He's going to be chained up downstairs, I know how upset you are. I can see it upon your face my dear. Everything will be alright now, I'm here." Allan said trying to embrace Maggie.

She broke away from him and ran to her room in tears. She cried for hours about poor Tepus.

Suddenly...

"BOOOOOOOOOOM"

A huge boulder smashed into the castle wall. Maggie looked outside to see an army advancing upon the castle. The soldiers of the kingdom all rushed out in hordes to fight the attackers.

"Oh god," Maggie was filled with fear, it was then that she knew she had to free Tepus and escape with him.

Maggie ran down the stairs, but quickly remembered a guard would be guarding the entryway to the staircase.

She quickly looked for the bricks that led to the end of the hallway she hadn't found with Tepus. She found it and quickly slid down the slope. She reached the trap door and took the same hard fall as before. This time Tepus would not break her fall. The princess was knocked senseless.

She slowly awakened. The room still reeked of the smell of sex. It even made her pussy wet from the smell. She then remembered her task, she ran down and into the dungeon where she found Tepus chained to a wall by his hands.

"Love!" Tepus weakly yelled.

"I'm here, Oh goodness how can I free you!" She yelled in a frightened state.

"I saw an axe down the hall you must try and get it!"

The sounds of battle could be heard outside the castle walls.

Maggie came dragging an axe which she struggle to put atop her shoulder

"Love I fear my aim will not be true." Maggie was crying.

"You must, I trust you, I love you." Tepus said looking at her, it only filled her with confidence as she weekly swung once, setting sparks flying. A second time and nothing. Finally a third time and she caught a weak link which freed his left hand. He then took the axe in one hand and freed himself of the other chains with it.

"Maggie look, I love you. So please go to your playroom and wait there until I come back!" Tepus urged her

"But but....we..." she stammered

"Go! Now!" he yelled as he ran out of the cell.

Allan of Gale was certainly out of place on this unexpected battlefield. Years away and fighting nothing but his imagination was proving his lack of worth now. He had mastered running and only helping out his fellow knights when he could. He attempted to help the valiant King as he fought off attacker after attacker.

Then out of the corner of his eye he saw the moor running shirtless with a battle axe in his powerful hand. Allan looked in fear as Tepus ran at him and with two hands swung the battle axe.

The axe whizzed past and Allan saw a horse fly by him carrying The lifeless attacker. He turned around to see Tepus continue to battle with the axe. He killed enemy after enemy while Allan began to advance behind him. Allan readied his sword and was about to stab the slave in the back when the worse happened.

"Allan!!!" The king yelled out as he fell to the ground his sword shielding him from an attacker's blade.

Allan simply turned around and proceeded to thrust at Tepus. When he missed, Tepus turned and swung the axe in a blind swing beheading Allan in a moment. Tepus then ran to the king and swung his axe into the attacker's side. He helped the King to his feet as they both fought off man after man. The attacker's finally began retreating as the two stood side by side watching.

Maggie suddenly came running towards them,

"Father, Tepus!" she yelled.

The King then saw an enemy cavalryman approaching his daughter. The king ran to her as did Tepus. The King grabbed his daughter and turned himself as the attacker dug his sword into the King. Tepus jumped and swung his axe, burying it into the side of the attacker.

The horse kept on riding with the lifeless man on its back. The King could only look at his daughter, his mouth agape. Tepus ran to them both and looked as the King muttered in his dying breath.......

"Watch over my daughter.......Brave Knight!" With that he fell to the ground.

Maggie fell over him, crying tears of utter despair. "Father no, nooooooo" her hands beating upon his body. She began to sob upon him when she felt Tepus arms on her shoulders. She buried her head in his chest as she continued to cry.

Tepus gently lifted her up and carried her back into the castle. She looked up with tear filled eyes as she brought her lips to his and they met in a soulful kiss.

"Take me to my room, love. please." Maggie cried, putting her head against his strong chest.

Tepus then carried her up the stairway and laid her upon her bed. She continued to cry as he stood at her window looking over the blood ridden battlefield which stretched for many acres beyond the castle walls. The castle forces had won but at great cost to both sides. In just a few short weeks, his world had totally changed and only his love for Magdelina was a certainty.

End of Volume 1

276

CPSIA information can be obtained
at www.ICGtesting.com
Printed in the USA
LVHW042010010821
694269LV00011B/1689